BILLIONAIRE AT THE CHRISTMAS INN

HANNAH JO ABBOTT

To my kids,
Phoebe, Phin, Asher, and Seth,
I love celebrating every day with you.

*C*hristmas was the last thing Logan Bradford wanted to think about. All the Christmas issues of the magazines he oversaw for the publishing company—one-hundred fifty-seven of them to be exact—had long been completed. And in his mind, Christmas was over and done with. Except for the actual day spent at his parents' house for Christmas dinner. But that would just be a day to eat too much food, and then he could go back to work.

So why was he staring at an email with a picture of an inn decorated top to bottom in greenery, lights, and Christmas wreaths? The only person that could convince him to think about this holiday was his mother, and she was begging him to join the family for a traditional Christmas tucked away in an inn in the North Carolina mountains.

Logan looked over the email that read: We haven't spent more than a few hours together as a family at Christmas in years. It's time. Please say you'll join us.

He leaned back in his desk chair and ran his hands over his dark hair. He liked it kept short, it was fast and easy, and he didn't have time to think about things like hair products.

He spun his chair around to stare out the floor-to-ceiling window of his high-rise office.

His mom meant well, of course. And could he really blame her for wanting her two sons together for the holiday? He rubbed his chin, remembering their Christmases as a kid. They had been full of fun and presents and good memories. But that's probably what his mom was hoping for. She wasn't likely to get that with Logan and his brother, both in their thirties, who barely spoke to each other, unless required by the business.

Logan sighed. A knock on the door interrupted him and he turned to watch his assistant enter.

"Mr. Bradford, your four o'clock appointment is in the lobby." She bit her lip. "And your mother is on line one."

He squeezed his eyes closed, knowing he wasn't getting out of this one. "Thanks. Give me two minutes and then show Mr. Jennings in." He collapsed into his desk chair and hit the button to answer the phone. "Hi, Mom." He took a deep breath. He knew by the end of the phone call, he would be going to a mountain inn for Christmas.

EVANGELINE PARKS LOVED EVERYTHING ABOUT CHRISTMAS. From the lights and decorations, to the music and the cookies, it was her most favorite season. But staring at the front of her inn, she felt a sense of overwhelm.

Still, she let out a happy sigh. Her own inn. Eva, as she had been known since she was little, had loved this place as a little girl, and when her grandmother, the original Evangeline, left it to her, she just knew it was the start of something special.

Of course, she hadn't known about the leaking roof and the rotting floorboards. It had taken months of hard work and all of her savings to get things ready in time for Thanksgiving. But the Inn was in good shape now. Just needed Christmas decorations. She had spent the last few days on a turkey hangover going through boxes in the attic. Unfortunately, only a few pieces were worth using. She would have to max out her credit card to buy new decorations. But it would be worth it. Bringing in guests for Christmas was going to be the thing that really got her business off the ground.

Now was one of the many moments when she wondered if she had bitten off more than she could chew. She nervously ran her fingers through her long, dark hair as she stared at the boxes of Christmas decorations in the yard and thought of the rest of them inside the house. Lewis, who worked at the property as a handyman and carry-heavy-things-guy, had offered to help with the outside garland and lights. But he was busy with a plumbing issue, and Eva didn't want to wait.

Sure, she had had to drag the extension ladder from the old shed, risking spider webs and other creatures she didn't want to think about. But this was her inn. *Her inn!* And she was going to see to it that every inch sparkled with Christmas cheer. She only hoped it wouldn't kill her.

*E*va groaned and pounded a hand against the counter. How could this be happening? She had a full house of guests arriving today, and she would need every ounce of energy to play multiple roles. One day, she might have a full staff, but on her shoestring budget, she was lucky to have Lewis and Sharon, the maid, and Joyce, the cook. Hiring anyone else was out of the question. So Eva worked as manager, hostess, check-in girl, and anything else that was needed.

Which is why she really needed her coffee this morning. Coffee that was made every morning in the industrial sized coffee maker. Sure, it might have been here since her grandparents bought the place, but it had never failed her before. So why was cold, murky water pouring in a stream into the coffee pot?

"Ugh!" She yelled. She grabbed a stool and stepped up to look inside the top. Of course, she didn't know what any of the inside parts were supposed to look like. But she grabbed the pot and went to the sink to fill it with more water. She returned and opened the lid. With the coffee pot full of water, she decided she needed new coffee grounds. In her frustration, she pulled out the coffee filter full of grounds with a little too much enthusiasm. She gasped as she realized what she was doing and tried to stop herself with the other hand. Too bad it held the pot of water.

"Ehh! What in the world?"

Eva's eyes grew wide as she turned to see that her first guest had indeed arrived. She had felt the coffee grounds and the water fly into the air. But she must have been too preoccupied to notice someone had walked in behind her. To her horror, she saw a man standing in her kitchen wearing what looked like an expensive silk dress shirt and several ounces of water and coffee grounds.

"I'm so sorry!" She frantically searched for a towel to clean up the mess. Without thinking, she ran to the man and started wiping the towel over his chest. When she glanced up at his face and saw him frozen like a statue and his eyes staring straight ahead, she realized she was inches away from him. "I'm uhh, I'm sorry. Here," she held out the towel, "You can have this." Her face flushed pink as she grabbed for another towel and began to clean up the floor. But she quickly realized the floor had been lucky. The guy had caught most of the mess.

"I'm sorry," she said for the third time. "I was just a little frustrated with the coffee maker, and I got a little upset. I guess I took it out on the kitchen." She gave a nervous laugh and looked to see if he possibly saw any humor in the situation.

His hard stare and grimace said he did not.

"We'll be happy to take care of your shirt. I can send it out to the dry cleaner today."

The man gave one last brush with the towel and handed it back to her. "That's not necessary."

"I'm Eva, are you checking in? I can help you with that."

"Yes, I didn't see anyone at the front desk, so I came in."

"Of course, that's fine. I'm sorry, I was just on my way out there, when I came to get coffee. And then... well," she held her arms out, indicating that he knew the rest of the story.

"I'll wait out front." He turned and went back the direction he had come in.

Once he was out of sight, Eva covered her face with her hands. How embarrassing. It was bad enough that she wasn't out front to greet him, but how was she going to face him out there now? She took several deep breaths and told herself to be a professional. And not to keep him waiting any longer.

Eva made her way to the foyer and put on a big smile as she entered. "Hello, I'm so sorry about all of that. Welcome to The Hideaway Inn."

"Bradford."

Eva lowered her eyebrows in confusion, but kept her smile perfectly placed. "Excuse me?"

"Bradford. The name on the reservation is Bradford."

"Oh, right. Great. I'll just look it up." With a few taps on the keyboard, she saw the reservation for four rooms. Perfect, the guy she threw coffee grounds on was her biggest reservation to date. "All right, Mr. Bradford, I've got you down for four rooms. When will the rest of your party be arriving?"

The front door swung open and the bell above it rang. The bell that should have alerted her that someone entered while she was in the kitchen. At least she knew now that it wasn't broken.

An older woman and man bustled in, "Is everything all right?" The woman asked. "It was taking a long time."

"Yes, everything's fine," the man at the desk said.

"Hello, welcome to The Hideaway Inn," Eva said again with her biggest smile. This was exactly how she had planned to greet her guests today. "Are you the Bradford party?"

"Yes, we are," the woman smiled brightly at Eva. "I'm Vickie and this is my husband Robert. And that," Vickie pointed at the man beside her, "is my son, Logan."

Son? Eva couldn't help herself, her eyes wandered over him and quickly checked for a ring on his left hand. Seeing none, she told herself to focus. "It's nice to meet you all. I'm Eva, and I'm here to make sure you have a wonderful visit. I have you down for four bedrooms, is that correct?"

"Yes, my younger son will be joining us later this evening. He had work he couldn't get away from this morning."

"Mother, she doesn't need our life story."

"Oh, it's fine, Logan, I was just explaining."

"That's fine. We like to treat our guests as family here, so we're happy to hear your story. I can show you up to your rooms. Do you have your luggage? I can send someone to carry it up."

"Oh no, no. No need for that. That's why I had boys." Vickie winked at her.

"Very well. I've got your room keys here. All of our rooms have king beds and are similar in size, but you're welcome to decide amongst yourselves who will stay in which room. Each one has a different theme that might suit you."

"Oh, I've already chosen. I looked at them online. We're staying in the White Christmas and Logan will be in the Christmas in Connecticut room and Jordan can stay in It's a Wonderful Life."

Eva beamed that Vickie had taken the time to look over the website and choose rooms. "Wonderful! I'm so glad you like them." She handed Vickie the first key. "Then this is yours." She turned to Logan and handed him a key, "And this is yours." She turned back to Vickie without meeting Logan's eyes. "Would you like me to keep Jordan's key at the front? Or give it to you?"

"I'll take it. He'll have to see me when he gets here that way."

Eva smiled. "I think we're going to get along just fine."

"I think so too," Vickie said.

"Right this way." Eva led them up the staircase that had just the right amount of creaking sound to it. She ran her hand along the real wood banister as she pointed out the features of the Inn. "The living room is just that way and is open anytime. There are books and DVDs and a piano if anyone plays. Past that is the kitchen. We serve breakfast, of course, so please let us know if you have any special dietary needs."

"Nope, no allergies for us. We love some good southern cooking," Vickie said.

"Wonderful." Eva felt herself sliding into her hostess role and she loved it. She could almost hear her grandmother's voice saying the same words. She had heard them enough as a child, and all the memories rolled back as she showed her guests around. "Here's the White Christmas room." She used her own master key and swung the door open.

Vickie gasped and put her hands to her mouth as she slowly walked into the room. "It's wonderful! Oh my, it actually smells like Christmas, it's like," she paused and sniffed the air, "Like vanilla and pine." She made her way around and touched the bedspread and the loveseat while her husband ambled along behind her and took a seat.

"Can I get you anything else?"

"Thank you, honey," Vickie said. "We'll just settle in and get our bags. I'm sure we'll see you downstairs later."

"Yes, ma'am. I'll be around if you need anything at all."

Eva cleared her throat, gathering her courage to face Logan now. "And now, I'll show you to the Christmas in Connecticut room." She walked past him, and couldn't be sure, but she thought she heard him scoff. She put on her smile as she opened the door.

Logan brushed past her, barely taking in the decor.

"Are you a fan of Christmas movies?" Eva asked.

Logan dropped his briefcase on the bed before he turned around. He scratched his head. "Apparently not as much as my mother."

"I hope you'll be very comfortable here. Please let us know if there's anything you need."

"Thanks," he turned and went to the window.

Eva pulled the door closed and as it clicked shut, she breathed a sigh of relief. She stood in the hallway for just a moment and tried to calm her nerves. She shook herself, remembering that she didn't have any time to waste.

She made her way back down the stairs and to the front desk. More guests could arrive at any minute. She didn't want to miss any more. Her mind again went to the coffee maker. Ugh. What was she going to do about that? No one wanted cold, yucky coffee. She grabbed the phone and dialed Lewis' number.

"Hey, boss lady."

"Hey, Lewis. Listen, there's something wrong with the coffee maker. Maybe it just had a bad morning. But it didn't heat the water at all."

"I'll take a look at it," he said in his delightful southern drawl.

"Thanks. Do you think there's another smaller coffee maker somewhere around here so we could make a regular pot in case we can't get that one going right away?"

"Sure, I think there's one in the back closet. I'll dig it out."

"Perfect. You're a saint."

Lewis laughed. "Far from it, but happy to help."

She hung up laughing, once again feeling thankful for Lewis. He had worked for her grandmother before she passed, and was probably in his late fifties now. The joke was that no one knew for sure how old he was. "I'm able-bodied, that's all that matters," he would say. Eva had to agree, since there was no task he couldn't handle.

Although, she suspected the coffee maker might be the thing to test that.

"Enough of that worry," Eva told herself. "You've got more guests coming in today. Just focus on one thing at a time." She didn't voice the rest of her thought, *And for goodness' sake, stop thinking about how handsome that guy looked even with coffee grounds on his shirt.*

*L*ogan collapsed onto the love seat in the over-decorated, Christmas-movie-themed room. If he had wanted to avoid Christmas, this was definitely the wrong place for that.

He ran a hand over his face and told himself not to be such a Scrooge. He was in the wrong room theme for that anyway. He didn't really hate Christmas, just didn't have time for all the frivolity of it. He reminded himself for the millionth time that this is what his mom wanted. And he wanted his mom to be happy.

He had been so distracted by the rooms in the inn that he forgot about his shirt. He took it off now and inspected it. It wasn't that bad, really. The coffee ground mostly just wiped off, and the water was already drying. It might need a little special attention, but nothing he didn't think would come out.

But what about this Eva? He couldn't help but wonder, what's her story? She seemed eager to please, and he wondered if she was afraid she might get fired for spilling coffee on him. He shook his head. He had been a boss long enough to know that there were things you fired people for and things you didn't.

Spilling coffee was not high on his list. Missing a deadline, losing marketing accounts, lying in an article, those were all serious offenses.

A knock on his door was followed by the sound of his mother's voice. "Logan? Are you in there?"

He stood and went to open the door.

"Are you ready to go get the luggage?" Vickie was practically glowing with happiness.

"Sure, mom."

"Isn't this place just wonderful?" She almost sang.

"It's nice," Logan said.

She looped her arm through his. "I just love it. I'm so glad we chose this particular inn. We're going to have a great time here with the whole family."

Logan gave her a smile. "Sure we will."

They made it down the stairs and Logan glanced at the desk as they walked through the front door. Eva smiled and waved, the phone was on her shoulder and she was typing in the computer.

Vickie waited until they were outside. "So what do you think of Eva?" Her eyes twinkled.

Logan shook his head slowly. "Mom, I'm not here to date anyone."

"Date?" Vickie asked, as if that was the last thing on her mind. "I didn't say 'date'. I just asked you what you think of her."

Logan scratched his head. He stopped himself from telling his mom about the coffee incident. No reason for her to know. "She seems eager to help. And she must like her job."

"Yes, she seems kind, and helpful. And very pretty."

"See?" Logan pointed an index finger at her. "I know what you're doing. I'm not here for that."

Vickie pouted. "But when are you going to find someone? You know I raised you boys and I loved it. Being a mother of boys was wonderful. But I'm ready to have a daughter now too. And I would like grandchildren someday."

Logan sighed. "It's not as easy as that. Especially in our family's line of work. I'm just busy with the company and I haven't met anyone that I'm ready to fall for." He left out his true thought that he hadn't found anyone he was ready to trust.

Vickie patted his arm. "Well, you might have to slow down sometime and actually look for someone. Don't wait too long, son. You don't want life to pass you by."

"Yes, ma'am," he said, placing a kiss on her cheek.

"Now then, let's get this luggage."

Vickie wasn't kidding when she said she needed sons to carry heavy things. She must have brought enough for a month.

"Your father's things are in here too," she explained.

"I'm sure Dad took up a whole half of one of these three suitcases."

She shrugged and smiled at him. "I just didn't want to forget anything."

"It's all right," he said, grunting as he lifted the bags. "I'm happy to help."

He was happy if his mom was happy. Still, he wasn't sure he would ever be able to give her the thing that would make her the happiest: a daughter-in-law.

"*D*id you get the syrup?" Eva asked as she helped Joyce set out breakfast the next morning.

"On the counter," Joyce called from the kitchen.

Eva made her way from the dining room and found the item. She sighed as she looked at Lewis standing over the coffee maker. "Still no luck?"

Lewis shook his head. "I'm sorry to say, no. I'm not sure why, but the heating element doesn't seem to be working."

"Can it be fixed?"

"Not sure."

"Can that part be replaced?" Eva asked hopefully.

"Not sure about that either. But I'll look into it. You know, my specialty is more physical than electrical."

Eva let her cheeks fill with air and then blew it out. She squeezed her eyes closed and told herself not to worry as she walked to the counter and poured the contents of the coffee pot into a thermos. She turned to make another pot in the small coffee maker. "This will have to do for today. But if we can't get it fixed, we'll have to get a new one." Dollar signs danced in her mind at the thought.

Lewis gave her a thumbs up sign. She knew by the look on his face that he wasn't confident it would work again.

Eva carried the syrup to the dining room and checked that the plates were set just right alongside the silverware and glasses.

"Wow, what a lovely table!" Vickie said as she entered the room. Robert, Logan, and a man Eva assumed must be the other son followed behind her.

"Thank you," Eva beamed at the praise.

"These dishes," Vickie gasped as she fingered the edge of a plate. "They're beautiful."

"They were my grandmother's. She used them here for years."

"So your grandmother owned the Inn?" Vickie asked.

"Yes, ma'am. She left it to me when she passed."

"Oh, I'm sorry for your loss. But what a gift."

"Yes," Eva let out a happy sigh. "Yes, it is."

Logan cleared his throat, and Eva noticed him in the corner.

"Why don't you folks take a seat and help yourself. I'm bringing in coffee. I'm sorry we're having to make it in small batches. Our bigger coffee maker decided to not work this morning."

The Bradford family took their seats and began passing pancakes, eggs, and bacon around the table.

Eva went to the kitchen and brought back the coffee. "Here you go, nice and hot."

"Eva," Vickie said.

"Yes, ma'am?"

"First of all, this is all delicious. Second of all, if you're having trouble with your coffee maker, maybe Logan could take a look at it. He's always been good at tinkering with things."

"Mother," Logan said through his teeth.

"What?" Vickie held her hands up. "You have been."

Eva watched his face and saw his clenched jaw and eyes darting back and forth. "Oh, really. It's fine. Our handyman has looked at it, and if we can't fix it, we'll just have to buy a new one." She felt sick to her stomach at the idea.

"Has your handyman been able to fix it?"

Eva bit her lip. "Well, no. Not yet."

"Then it won't hurt anything if Logan takes a look. Who knows, maybe he can figure it out." Vickie flashed a smile and her eyes twinkled as if she was planning something.

"Sure," Jordan spoke up for the first time. "Logan, superhero of all things, can swoop in and fix the coffee maker too."

Eva watched as Logan glared at him. "It's not being a superhero to just show up and do your job like a responsible adult."

"Boys, not here," Robert said.

There was an awkward pause before Vickie raised her eyebrows, tilted her head and said, "Logan?"

He sighed. "Sure. I'll take a look."

"Thanks," Eva mumbled, afraid she had stumbled into a family dispute and didn't want to cause any more problems. "No rush. Anytime today is fine."

"I'll do it after breakfast," Logan said.

"Great. Thank you. Enjoy your breakfast everyone." Eva headed back to the kitchen and told her heart to stop pounding like it was going to come out of her chest. She didn't like conflict, and she didn't like being a burden to her guests who were supposed to enjoy themselves.

Eva kept herself busy the rest of breakfast. She greeted other guests as they came downstairs, but tried to stay out of the dining room. Of course, she wasn't avoiding anyone. She just had things to do. Lots of things. Like straighten the front desk, dust the bookshelves, and drink three cups of coffee.

No new guests were checking in today. In fact, they were

almost full. Eva laughed to herself thinking there was no room at the inn. Except there was one room. But that was all, for the next two weeks solid. Her work on the website and online advertising really seemed to be paying off. She stopped in the living room after she finished dusting the bookshelves and looked over the small portrait of her grandparents on the back wall. The black-and-white photo had been taken shortly after their wedding. Eva smiled seeing their happy faces. They were so in love. Her grandmother always said they had no idea what they were doing, but they had each other and that was enough.

It had been enough to survive on a small income for years before her grandfather got a good job with the city. Then they saved their pennies to buy an inn they could run together. It had been their dream.

Eva ran her hand over the picture, before making her way back to the kitchen. She only hoped she would make them proud.

LOGAN STUFFED HIS HANDS IN HIS POCKETS AND LET OUT A BIG breath. Why did his mother always push him into things like this? He would never volunteer to help a stranger. Especially at the place they were paying to stay. Not that the money was that important. Logan didn't usually think much about having ten digits in his bank account. It had been a part of his life for a long time. Maybe he took it for granted sometimes, but mostly he just went to work every day like a normal guy. Sure, maybe he had more expensive suits and cars, but he never planned to sit around and get comfortable with his money.

He also didn't exactly plan to fix coffee makers in small inns as a side project either. But he knew his mom was right when she said he could probably figure it out. And he didn't want to be rude now that she had volunteered him. He figured now was as good a time as any.

He walked purposefully into the kitchen. No one was there and he breathed a sigh of relief. Maybe he could get in and fix it without having to talk to anyone. He stepped to the counter and took the lid off the machine. He was just peering into the top when he heard footsteps. So much for not talking.

"Oh hey," the sound of Eva's voice made him turn to glance at her. "Thanks for taking a look. But really, no pressure. We can figure something out if it doesn't work."

Logan furrowed his eyebrows. "So you don't think I can fix it?"

Eva pressed her lips together and lifted both palms towards the ceiling. "I have no idea. Is this the kind of work you do?"

Logan let out a laugh. "Fixing coffee makers?"

Eva laughed too. "Not specifically, but I mean do you work with machines or something?"

"No, not at my job. But I do tinker with things for fun."

"Huh," Eva chuckled. "That's nice. I don't have much time for fixing things as a hobby."

Logan shrugged. "It's nice to have something to challenge my brain sometimes." He heard a stool scrape across the floor and looked to see that she had taken a seat and propped her elbow on the counter. Her chin rested in her hand.

"So what do you do for a living?" she asked.

There it was. How much could he tell the truth without revealing everything? He had been clear with his parents and his brother that he didn't want anyone on the trip to know what their family did. It only made people act differently around them. Or made them a target. "I work in publishing.

But really I just sit in an office all day." There. That was true and didn't say too much.

"Publishing? That sounds interesting. What kind of publishing?"

"Magazines."

"Oh, cool. What magazine?"

He almost wanted to laugh. Which one? There wasn't one. There were hundreds. But in that moment, he realized that was his out. "Southern Hunting and Fishing." Surely she couldn't have much interest in that.

"Really?" Eva's eyes went wide. "My grandfather always read that magazine."

"Nice." Inwardly he groaned.

"We probably still had copies of it lying around."

Logan's heart skipped a beat.

"But I threw out all that kind of stuff when I took over." Eva let out a laugh. "My grandparents never threw anything away."

Logan breathed easier. He would hate for her to go digging and find his family's company listed in the magazine. Sure, it said "Hometown American Publishing," but two clicks on Google would tell her the company was owned by the Bradford family. He cleared his throat and attempted a change in subject. "How long have you been working here?" He turned his attention back to the coffee machine as she answered.

"I followed my grandmother around all over the place as a child. So she started giving me 'jobs' around the inn when I was about five. Then I had a paying job in the summers and holidays as a teenager. But I lived here full time."

"With your grandparents?" He asked, but didn't turn to look at her. He reached down to find where the heating coil connected at the bottom of the machine.

"Yeah, with my grandparents."

He thought he detected a note of sadness, but told himself to focus. He'd only asked to keep her talking about herself and not him.

"Then I went to college and after I graduated, I worked at a marketing firm for a while. My grandfather got sick and died not long after that. My grandmother couldn't keep the place going. Honestly I think she just didn't have the heart to do it without him. And then she passed away two years ago."

"I'm sorry," Logan said. He turned to see her shrug and give him a smile that said she was all right.

"So I came back here. I spent some time getting things back in shape and then worked on marketing and promoting for the inn. My grandparents started out small, so they always depended on word-of-mouth advertising. They barely knew what the internet was. But I knew if I was going to get the place on the market, I needed to go big with our online presence."

Logan closed the lid on the coffee maker and turned to face her. "That's smart," he said. "Advertising is important, and online marketing is everything now." He had meant it as a compliment, but her face twisted in concern. "What? Did I say something wrong?" He suddenly felt terrible that he had hurt her feelings.

She pointed behind him. "So is it dead. Forever?"

"What?" He scrunched his eyebrows in confusion. "Oh, the coffee maker?"

"Yeah." She bit her lip as she waited for his answer.

"No, it's fixed."

"What?" Eva jumped down off the stool. She clapped her hands once as her face lit up with a smile. "Are you serious?"

"Yep. The heating coil must have shorted. So I reset it. But the fuse probably needs to be replaced. That's a pretty simple repair, though."

"Wow," Eva stood with her mouth hanging slightly open.

She only stood for a minute before she started jumping up and down. "Thank you."

Logan thought she looked like she wanted to hug him. He took a step back, but only bumped into the counter. "Yes, well. You're welcome." He reached out and shook her hand like he had just closed a business deal. "See you later." He turned and walked out.

As he rounded the corner, he found his mom and dad coming down the steps.

"Hi, we're going to go explore some of the shops in town. Want to join us?" Vickie asked.

"Maybe next time. I'm going to my room for a little while."

"Suit yourself. You'll miss out on all the fun." She sang on her way out the door.

Logan shook his head. He loved his mom, but his idea of fun wasn't the same as hers. He went to his room and closed the door. The silence was comforting. He could feel safe where no one would ask him intrusive questions.

He pulled a book from the shelf and sat on the love seat. Every time he glanced up from the pages, he could see the gorgeous view out the window.

Logan told himself to focus on the words on the page and not think of the look on Eva's face as she thanked him. And how adorable she had been in her excitement over such a little thing as a coffee maker.

*E*va stood at the front desk and tapped her pencil on the pad of paper she held. She was making a list. Or at least she was supposed to be. But something kept distracting her.

That something was a six-foot-tall, dark-headed man who had single-handedly saved her coffee maker. And by extension, maybe her whole inn.

The bell over the front door jingled and reminded her to do her job. She smiled at the guests returning from a walk and let them know there was hot coffee in the kitchen.

She shook her head and turned her attention to her list. There were supplies to buy, and Lewis said a delivery had come and he needed to know where to put it. She knew it was extra Christmas decorations that she had ordered. She would have to put them up later. "Focus," she whispered to herself. And that was enough to convince herself. She spent the next thirty minutes making a supply list on her pad and then made a list of things she needed to check on or handle before she made the trip to town to purchase the items.

Her cell phone rang just as she was finishing her list. "Hey, Katie," she said to her friend.

"Hey, girl, have you seen the news?"

"What news?"

"About the weather."

Eva furrowed her eyebrows in concern. "No, what are you talking about?"

"You need to check the forecast. They're saying we could get snow on Thursday. Like a lot of snow."

"Really?" Eva's voice actually squeaked in excitement.

"Yeah, but Eva, I'm not sure it's good. They're saying it could be a big storm. Ice and snow on the ground."

"What? We don't usually get that much snow in December. Are you sure you heard right?"

"Yep. Go check it out. They're talking like the snowstorm of 2009."

Eva's mouth fell open. "Oh no," her first thought was all her guests. "I was headed to pick up supplies this afternoon."

Katie gasped. "You better go now. The stores are going to be crazy with people stocking up."

Eva didn't waste any time. "I'll go right now. Thanks for the heads up."

"No problem. I wanted to make sure you knew. Be careful."

Eva smiled at the concern in her friend's voice. "Will do. Gotta run." She opened the computer and did a quick check of the news. Katie was right. They were used to a light dusting this early, but snowstorms like this only happened once in a blue moon. But according to the weather man, this was that blue moon.

She ran to her room and grabbed her purse. She asked Sharon to keep an eye on the front desk in case anyone needed anything, then she looked for Lewis. She found him coming around the back of the yard.

"Eva," he said before she could get a word in. "Did you hear the weather report?"

"Katie just called to tell me about it. I'm leaving now to go to town for supplies. I hope I'm not too late."

"I'll make a few preparations here. We've got extra blankets in every nook and cranny of this place. And there's a generator in the garage, but I'll get extra gas just in case."

"Thanks, Lewis. I'll check in with you before I head back." Eva was already in preparation mode. She couldn't help the worry seeping in for her guests' safety...and for their basic needs of food and supplies. The list she had made now seemed like only a fraction of what she might need. But she knew if the stores were crowded, she might not get everything on her list. She sighed as she jumped in her car and headed down the mountain. She would just have to do the best she could do.

Still, she felt the smile that she couldn't wipe off her face. It might be scary, but the thought of snow sounded magical, and her full inn right in the middle of the Christmas season was ready for a bit of magic.

*L*ogan stared at his computer screen with his head down. The weather report didn't look good. He read a few more lines to make sure he understood before he stood to go find his family.

Just as he shut his door behind him, Jordan came out of his own room across the hall.

"Hey, Bro, what's up?" Jordan asked, as if he cared.

"I just read the weather report. Looks like a bad snowstorm is coming. I'm going to find Mom and Dad to tell them."

Jordan rubbed his scruffy face. "Huh. Snow doesn't sound so bad."

Of course he would think that. "It can be dangerous if it knocks out the power and we can't go anywhere."

Jordan held his hands out in the air. "Where would you want to go? We're all here in the mountains on vacation. Would getting stuck be that bad?"

Logan left out a huff. He didn't expect his younger brother to be concerned. About anything. "I'm going to find Mom and Dad," he repeated.

"I'll come with you."

The two descended the stairs, but they didn't have far to go, since Vickie and Robert were in the living room. They sat near the fireplace, both holding mugs of coffee.

"Hey there, we were just wondering where you two were," Robert said. "There's coffee if you want some. I'm assuming that's compliments of Logan."

Logan only nodded briefly before getting to his mission. "I was just reading the news." He explained about the weather situation. "It's supposed to arrive on Thursday, just two days from now."

Vickie and Robert didn't move from their seats. When they gave no response, Logan spoke again. "Did you hear me? We could be sitting in several inches of snow, maybe a foot or more if the predictions are right."

Vickie smiled. "We heard you. But what do you want us to do?"

Logan cleared his throat. "I think we should go home."

"Go home?" Vickie raised her voice. "We just got here! We're supposed to be enjoying family time together. For Christmas." She emphasized the last word.

Logan sighed. "I know. But we could get stuck here, and we might not have power or food."

Vickie waved a hand. "Oh, I'm sure Eva has taken care of things. We won't starve. And we'll be here together. It will be a bonding experience."

Logan knew he wasn't going to win this one. "Fine. But don't say I didn't warn you."

Vickie stood and patted her son on the arm. "Don't worry so much. We'll be just fine. Maybe it will just turn out to be our best Christmas ever."

He doubted that, but what else could he do?

"Now then," Vickie said, pointing to each of her sons in turn. "No more of this hiding-out-in-your-rooms thing.

We're here to be together and enjoy this beautiful place. So let's go out and see some of the town, just in case we're stuck here later in the week. Okay?"

Jordan was the first to agree. "Okay."

"Okay," Logan mumbled. The four of them grabbed coats and necessities for the next few hours and loaded into the car. Logan tried to enjoy the time with them, following his mom around the quaint shops in town, walking through the tourist areas down the mountain. They ate lunch at a café, and Vickie fawned over her salad and announced multiple times how good the bread was. She was right, of course. But all Logan could think about was being trapped in a tiny inn with people he didn't know. Without necessities or power, that could be very interesting. He didn't mind being with his family, but he had no desire to bond with other people he'd never met before.

ON WEDNESDAY NIGHT, LOGAN COULDN'T SLEEP. THE weather man was still predicting this to be a severe snowstorm, and Logan stood at the window in his bedroom, as if he was going to watch it come right up to the inn. The last two days had been enjoyable for the most part. But now, he couldn't help but wish he was at his own home. It might not snow as bad there. But even if it did, he would be surrounded by familiar things. And he would be alone. He could get along just fine for a few days without talking to anyone. There were books to catch up on and things to think about. But here? What was he going to do here? Maybe he could read, but his mother wouldn't let him "hide out" in his room as she called it. Why was it so bad to want to spend time alone?

He finally went to bed and closed his eyes. But he felt

certain he could hear the wind bringing in the snow as he fell asleep.

7

*E*va stood in the dining room grasping her coffee cup and staring out the window in pure excitement. "Snow," she whispered. Just as expected, it had arrived first thing this morning. She was up early and crept to the window before her eyes were completely open to see if the ground was covered in white. It wasn't quite yet at that time, but now as she was getting ready for her guests to come down for breakfast, the white flakes were coming down steadily. She knew the rest of the day might be perilous if it kept up, so for now she planned to let herself enjoy it.

"Good morning," Vickie called out quietly. She made her way to the window and stood close to Eva. "Isn't it just beautiful?" she asked.

Eva nodded. "I think so."

"I could just cuddle up in a chair and watch this all day."

Eva turned to her and smiled. "Well, why don't you? It looks like it's going to be here for a while. You should enjoy it."

Vickie patted her shoulder. "I just might do that. And what about you?"

"Oh, I wish. I've got too much to do today. But I'm glad I got a few minutes to watch it this morning. I think snow always brings a little bit of magic."

Vickie beamed. "Me too. What kind of snow magic are you hoping for today?"

Eva swallowed her emotions, as the question surprised her. What did she really hope for? To keep her inn, to honor the memory of her grandparents, to find her own happiness the way they did. She couldn't say most of that to her paying guest. She shrugged. "Just for a Merry Christmas, I guess."

"I'm sure you'll get just that," Vickie winked.

When Vickie said it, it felt like it might be true. "I hope everyone here will have a Merry Christmas. You and your family included."

"I'm sure we will too, so don't you worry about that. This is the longest time we've spent together in a very long time. So in my book, it's already the best Christmas I can imagine."

That was Eva's Christmas magic. Maybe her own happiness lie in making others happy here at her inn. Her own family might not have been what she would have wished for as a child. But she could provide a place for other families to make happy memories together.

She cleared her throat. "Well, I better get to work if we want a warm breakfast on the table. I'm planning to let all the guests know, but we'll be serving lunch and dinner today because of the snow. And we'll make a plan for the next few days as we see what the weather decides to do."

"That sounds just fine. I'm sure you've got everything under control."

Eva hoped she did. She gave Vickie a smile as she headed to the kitchen to help bring out the plates and food.

Not long after, most of the guests had come down and helped themselves to breakfast. But no one was interested in sitting at the dining room table. Everyone seemed content to grab a plate of food and find themselves a spot to watch the snow. Eva peeked in the living room to see that Vickie had secured a coveted spot next to the large picture window. It was exactly the spot Eva had sat in to watch snow as a girl.

Eva wished she could snuggle up in that spot today. But she needed to check on her staff and go over the plans for the day. She had been fortunate the day she went supply shopping to get everything on her list and stock up on extra groceries so they could provide extra meals for the guests. Even though she knew if they got stuck for a few days, those meals might be peanut butter and jelly sandwiches. At least no one would go hungry.

After she spoke with Sharon and Lewis and Joyce, she did a quick check on all the rooms and let the guests know about their meal plans. Once that was all done, she found herself with time she didn't know what to do with. No guests to check in. No one going out, and it wasn't time to prepare lunch yet. An idea struck her and as she remembered what her grandmother would do on snow days. She headed to the kitchen to recreate a Christmas memory.

She stood on a stool to reach the top cabinet. In the very back corner there was a small box, covered in yellow flower paper. She had to stand on her tiptoes to reach it. She just had it in her fingertips and managed to pull it out.

"Woah, what are you doing?" Logan's voice close by startled her and she flinched, causing her to lose her balance.

"Ahh," she screamed as she tipped off the side of the stool. She just knew she was going to crash on the floor when she felt herself caught in the grasp of strong arms. She coughed as the impact of landing on his chest hit her. She was too shocked to say anything, but she watched as the cards from the box she had pulled out flew in the air and fell to the floor like the snowflakes outside the window. She glanced back to see Logan's eyes wide and his mouth slightly open. "I...I...I'm so sorry," she finally muttered. Her heart pounded as she realized how close her face was to his.

He seemed to come out of his shock and set her down gently on the floor. "No, I think it was my fault. I didn't mean to scare you. But that stool looked precarious."

Eva let out a laugh that sounded nervous even to her. "I guess it was. But I was just reaching for my grandmother's recipe box." She dropped her gaze to the papers all around the floor.

"Oh no, I'm sorry. I can help you put them back. I hate that they're out of order now."

Eva laughed again at that. "Actually, no. There are little dividers in it with different categories, but my grandmother never seemed to put them back. She just stuck them in the front when she was done, so they're all out of order anyway. But I know the recipe I'm looking for is on a red piece of paper. It's typed, but then glued onto the red. This might even make it easier to find it."

Logan gave her an incredulous look. "If you say so."

"Yep, I do. Here, help me look." She squatted down and started digging through the cards. He seemed unsure, but followed suit.

For several minutes they worked in near silence, picking up cards and checking for red paper. "Is this it?" Logan asked.

Eva squinted as she looked at the paper. "Yes!" She grabbed the card and held it triumphantly in the air. "Thank you!"

"You're welcome." He stood and brushed his hands off, even though he had been looking through clean cards and not dirt. "What's the recipe?"

"My grandmother's secret chocolate chip recipe."

"Oh. Chocolate chip cookies are my favorite."

Eva watched his face and he seemed to have surprised himself by saying that.

"Really? Mine too. Would you like to help me bake them?"

He looked at her with a strange expression, as if he couldn't quite decide what to say. He finally gave a short laugh. "I can't remember the last time I baked cookies."

"Who's baking cookies?" Vickie said, entering the kitchen. "Oh my." Her eyes traveled to the contents of the recipe box that were still on the floor. "What happened?"

"Oh, it's fine. Just a little accident." Eva said. "I fell off the stool and dropped the box."

Vickie's eyes grew wide. "Are you all right?"

"Just fine." Without thinking, Eva patted her hand on Logan's chest, "Logan caught me."

Vickie looked from Eva to Logan and back again, a surprised look still on her face. "Well, then. You are a hero," she said.

"Right?" Eva agreed. "First my coffee maker, now me. And he even found my grandmother's cookie recipe."

"So you're going to bake cookies with Eva?" Vickie pressed her lips together in a grin as her eyes twinkled.

"What?" Logan asked. "No, I just um. I just came in to check on the coffee maker."

"You're welcome to help with the cookies if you'd like. Everyone should bake cookies once in a while. If you can't remember the last time, then it's probably time."

"Sure!" Vickie clapped her hands. "What a wonderful way to spend a snowy day. I'll leave you to it. But I'll be looking forward to cookies when they come out of the oven."

8

*L*ogan knew what his mother was doing. Eva might not, and his mother might pretend that she didn't know, but he could see it. She was back to her matchmaking. Really, just pushing people together is what she called it. But he knew. She somehow had a knack for saying just the right thing to get people to spend time together. And she had set her sights on Eva the first day they walked into this place.

Maybe it wouldn't be so bad. He did like chocolate chip cookies. And Eva was nice enough. As long as he could steer her away from personal subjects, and stop admitting things, like his favorite dessert.

"Okay, here's the deal though." Eva leaned back into the corner of the counter and pressed the recipe against her chest. "This is a secret family recipe. If I reveal the special ingredient, you have to promise not to tell anyone."

"Sure," he said. Keeping secrets was something he was good at.

"I guess we better clean up these cards first." She began scooping up the cards and putting them in the box.

"Don't you want to put them in order now? Seems like a good opportunity."

"Nah," Eva said. "My grandmother's way worked pretty well for her all those years. Why change tradition?"

"To be more efficient?" he asked.

Eva tilted her head. "I probably would have said the same thing. But with my grandmother, everything wasn't just about making good time." She stood as if thinking for a few moments. "I guess if I had to describe it, it was more like making time. She made time for baking and cooking, for taking care of the inn, and for people. If I needed her, she was always there. So baking or looking for a recipe might take a little time, but it was time she always seemed to make for what was important."

Logan watched her expression as she spoke. He could tell she cared deeply for her grandmother and the time they shared. Maybe there was something to be said for taking time instead of making good time. He held out a handful of recipe cards to her. "Here's to making time," he said.

Eva stacked them up and then turned and placed the red card on the counter. "Here we go. Now, all the baking goods are in the pantry there. But here's the secret ingredient. Come close, I can't say it too loud."

Cautiously, he stepped up to the counter next to her and leaned down slightly. She cupped her hand over his ear and he felt the soft skin of her hand graze his face. He caught the scent of vanilla.

"We ground up a Hershey's chocolate bar to mix in."

He straightened, feeling surprised that he was reluctant to move away from her. "Really? I've never heard of that before."

Eva nodded with a look of pride. "Mmhmm, trust me. You're going to love it."

With one glance, he felt like maybe he could trust her. She

just offered up her family secret. Did that mean she was taking him into her confidence? Or that she was happy to blab secrets to anyone?

"I'll be the judge of that," he said.

Eva laughed. "Oh, I'm sure you will. Let's get started." She went to the pantry for the first ingredients and he followed her lead. He looked over the recipe and went to the pantry to see what he could carry. When she turned around carrying flour and sugar, she bumped into him with an "Oof".

"Sorry," he said.

"No problem," Eva went around him to the counter as he searched for baking powder and chocolate chips.

For several minutes they performed an awkward dance of back and forth into the small pantry and back to the counter. But at last they had all the ingredients they needed.

Eva opened a bottom cabinet and lifted out a kitchen mixer. "Here," she said. "I'll start mixing the dry ingredients and you can crack the eggs."

"All right." He took a bowl from the cabinet and began his task. He thought they were falling into a comfortable silence. But Eva had other ideas.

"Want to turn on some Christmas music?" She asked.

He narrowed his eyes at her. "Do you?"

"Sure," she shrugged. "Why not? It's Christmas time. It's snowing, and we're making cookies. What's more Christmas than that?"

"I'm guessing all of that while listening to Christmas music."

She smiled and wiggled her eyebrows up and down. "Exactly." She picked up her phone and scrolled across the screen. "Oh, here we go," she said. The sound of Bing Crosby's voice came out of a speaker in the corner of the kitchen. "White Christmas seems appropriate."

"You really do like Christmas movies, don't you?" Logan asked.

Eva smiled. "Of course, who doesn't?" She gave him a look. "Don't you?"

Logan shrugged. "I don't really watch a lot of tv or movies. So the holiday variety doesn't thrill me much."

She stared at him with her mouth slightly open. "But you have seen White Christmas, right?"

"Maybe as a kid. I don't remember, though."

"Christmas in Connecticut?"

Logan shook his head.

"It's a Wonderful Life?"

He looked at her curiously. "Are you just naming rooms in your inn?"

She punched him in the arm. "No. They're all Christmas movies."

"Yeah, I've heard of them." He turned his attention to the eggs. "But you're listing all the ones in your inn."

"I know, because they're my favorite."

"Hmm. Well, I think I've seen a few of them. But not lately, and they didn't stick in my memory."

"Well we might have to fix that problem."

"I don't see it as a problem." He lifted the bowl he held. "Are you ready for the eggs?"

She seemed to have forgotten about the cookies. "Oh, sure." She scooted over the bowl with the dry ingredients and waited for him to pour in the eggs. "You know, I have all those movies on DVD in the living room. You just might force me to host a Christmas movie marathon if we get snowed in."

He scrunched his eyebrows as if that might be painful. "Who uses DVDs anymore?" He immediately wished he could take it back when he saw the hurt look in her eyes.

She turned her back as she stirred the ingredients. "I

haven't had the funds to put streaming devices in all the rooms. My grandparents put DVD players in the room a few years ago. It was a major expense at the time. But guests seemed to really appreciate it."

"Of course," he said. "I'm sure the DVDs are welcome."

He noticed how she straightened her shoulders and lifted her chin. "It's what we have. So we make it work." She turned to check the temperature on the oven.

Logan let his eyes linger as she pushed her long, dark ponytail behind her shoulder. He had noticed she hadn't mentioned any parents, and he knew her grandparents were gone. Did she have anyone else? He admired the way she held her own, even to his unkind comment. She must have worked very hard to get the inn to the full capacity that it was at this very moment. He racked his brain to think of something to say. But he'd never been great at encouragement, or at saying the right thing. "Cookies were a good idea." He said, feeling lame.

She turned and flashed a smile, seeming to bounce back quickly. "I think so too. The guests will like them. Plus, we have now rectified your lack of baking time, for a little while at least."

Logan smiled despite himself. "Yes, that's true." They went about rolling the dough into balls and placing it on cookie sheets. "So do you use the Christmas theme year round?"

"Oh no," Eva said, rolling dough between her fingers. "It's actually something new I tried for the holiday season. I thought it would be fun."

Logan nodded slowly. "Seems like a smart business decision."

"Thanks. Usually the rooms are actually named for literary figures."

"Really?" That perked his interest. "Which ones?"

"The room you're staying in is Charles Dickens."

Logan almost dropped the dough. "You're kidding."

Eva turned and gave him a look that said she wasn't sure if he was being sarcastic or not. "No, that's the name of the room."

"My favorite author."

"Really?" Eva lit up. "Huh, how about that."

"How about that," Logan repeated thoughtfully. "Who else?"

"Emily Dickinson, Jane Austen, Mark Twain, Ernest Hemingway, William Faulkner, Louisa May Alcott."

Logan nodded. "All solid names." He smiled. "I have to be honest, that sounds more up my alley than Christmas movies."

Eva laughed. "I can understand that. I like movies, but my grandmother named the rooms years ago. I have no desire to change them permanently."

"Good to hear."

"Finished?" Eva asked.

Logan turned to her and their eyes met. For a moment he had no idea what she was talking about. He had been busy trying to keep to himself and ignore the Christmas around him. But this had been fun. Maybe more fun than he'd had in a while. And it was because of her. He felt comfortable as they chatted, and that was really saying something. Her eyes, though, the deepest shade of chocolate brown he had ever seen. He felt like there was so much more behind them than Christmas decorations and silly movies.

"With the cookies," Eva said, clearing up the confusion.

"Oh, yes. All done." He slid the baking sheet towards her.

"Perfect. I'll just pop these in the oven." She did so and then brushed her hands off. "Mmm, I can't wait to try them." She turned to him and he saw the bit of dough on her cheek.

"You umm, you have something." He pointed to his own cheek to indicate.

"Oh," she felt for it but missed. "Did I get it?" She asked.

"No, it's higher."

She tried again, with no success. "There?"

"No, not quite." He hesitated, but knew it was the only thing to do, and surprisingly it felt just right. He reached out and swiped her cheek with his finger. Her skin was as soft as it looked. He held up the smear of dough for her to see.

Logan watched Eva blush before turning to clean up the kitchen. But what stayed with him was the way his heart was pounding from the encounter.

9

*E*va watched out the window at the heavy snow that she had been excited about a few days before. The weather report had been correct, and they had received several inches of snow. Thankfully, they had kept their power so far, a fact that Eva had whispered a prayer of thanks for every morning. But now that she, her staff, and all their guests had been stuck at the inn for four days, their supplies were beginning to run low.

Starting with their supply of coffee. Eva had grossly underestimated the amount they would need to caffeinate that number of people. She glanced at her own coffee cup, now empty, wishing for a second cup, but knowing she couldn't have one.

That made her decision. She would have to go into town for supplies. From all reports, the roads around town had been cleared. It was only the roads down the mountain that would be dangerous. But she had a responsibility, and she needed to feed everyone.

She sighed as she took one last glance over the pure white ground that surrounded her inn before she turned to find

Lewis. She found him in the kitchen, staring at the coffee maker.

"I'm glad we got this thing working again. But didn't know we might not have a use for it now."

"I know, it's a shame." Eva nodded at him. "I'm hoping to rectify that today."

Lewis tipped his head and gave her a stern look. "Does that mean you have developed the ability to fly?"

"Nope."

"So you've called in the National Guard and they're delivering coffee?"

"Not that either."

"Because I know you can't mean you are planning to drive to get coffee."

"Not just coffee," she explained. "We're running low on everything. The stores in town are open. I might not get top pick or a variety of choices, but I can get food, and coffee."

Lewis shook his head. "I don't think that's a good idea. It's not safe for you to drive down the mountain with the current conditions."

"Who's driving down the mountain?" Vickie entered the kitchen, her tone disapproving already. She seemed to have a way of hearing the most important news from whatever room she was in.

Eva cleared her throat and reminded herself that she was an adult and she was in charge here. "I am."

Vickie's eyes grew wide. "Is that a good idea?"

"No," Lewis said, giving Eva a look.

"It will be fine. I grew up here, I've driven in the snow plenty of times. But I have to. We need food and supplies."

Vickie sighed. "Are you sure? Could we make it another day or two?"

Eva shook her head. "No, it needs to be today. If I can

make the trip worthwhile, then we'll be fine for a while longer. But I'll have to go."

"Let me," Lewis said.

Eva held up a hand. "No, it's my responsibility and I can handle it."

Vickie's eyes grew wide before her expression changed and a grin spread across her face. "I have an idea. Let Logan go with you."

Eva felt her cheeks grow warm. Why did that happen? Logan was just a guest, nothing more. Wasn't he? "Oh no, that's not necessary."

"Oh, I insist," Vickie said. "It might be all right, but you have to admit that it's precarious out there, and if you're going out to get supplies to feed our family, I would feel better if Logan went with you. It's not a good idea to be alone out there, just in case something happens."

Eva sighed. She wanted to handle this on her own. So why did the idea of Logan going with her make her feel a little safer? And why did she hope that he actually wanted to go too? "Well, if you insist. But I don't want to pull him away from anything. Maybe we should ask him first."

Vickie waved a hand in the air. "Oh, it's no problem. What else can he be doing?" She laughed. "I'll go up and get him now."

"Oh, I'm not quite ready to go yet." Eva subconsciously patted her hair with the sudden urge to look in a mirror.

"That's all right. I'll just tell him to be ready and you'll knock on his door when you're ready to go." Vickie fluttered out of the room before Eva could say anything else.

Eva stood staring after her. Her mind racing in twenty different directions—what did she need to buy, which store should she go to first, what would Logan think about her outfit?

Lewis patted her shoulder and it brought her back to the

moment. He gave a light laugh. "It will be just fine. I have no doubt."

She scrunched her eyebrows as she turned to look at him. Unsure if he meant the safety of the roads, or spending the time alone with a handsome guest.

Thirty minutes later, Eva had made a detailed list, checked her hair in the mirror and bundled up in her winter coat, hat, and gloves. She raised her hand to knock on Logan's door and quickly tapped three times. It was only a few seconds before the door opened and Logan stood in front of her. He wore dark jeans and a dark green sweater. "Hi," was all he said.

"Hi," Eva returned the greeting. "I guess you heard your mom volunteered you for a mission."

He grinned. "Yes, I did."

But he didn't say he was happy about it. "Of course, please don't feel any pressure, if you don't want to go, I'll be fine on my own."

He gave her a look that she wasn't sure about. Had she hurt his feelings? Did he actually want to go? Either way, he didn't say.

"But I'm happy to have the company, if you're up for adventure."

Logan raised his eyebrows. "I'm not big on adventure. But you may have noticed not a lot of people can say no to my mother. Also, I don't mind."

Eva smiled, certain that was as much as she was going to get from him. He had been at her inn for a week now, and he was still a mystery to her. "In that case, I guess we better get going."

He turned to pick up his coat and then stepped into the hallway and pulled the door closed behind him. Eva forgot to step backwards, and now she stood inches from him. She could smell his cologne, a lovely deep-woodsy kind of smell.

She was tempted to stand there and take in another deep breath. But she caught herself in time and stepped back towards the stairway.

Logan held a hand out in the air. "After you," he said.

Eva turned and managed to make it down the stairs without any more awkward social blunders. She turned to Sharon at the front desk and said, "I shouldn't be gone for more than a couple of hours. But call if you need anything, or if you think of anything else I need to pick up in town."

Sharon gave her a thumbs up. "Don't worry. We'll be fine here. Just be careful."

"I will." Eva opened the front door and Logan followed her out to the porch. They carefully walked down the snow-covered steps and made their way to the garage. As they neared the truck, Logan held out his hand to her. She gave him a curious look.

"Keys?" he asked.

It took her a moment to understand. "To the truck?"

He nodded.

"Oh, I'll drive."

Logan stopped walking and his eyes were serious as he said, "Please, let me."

She forced herself to laugh, so she wouldn't sound too defensive. "I can handle it. I've driven down the mountain plenty of times. I grew up here, remember?"

Logan took in a deep breath and let it out slowly. He seemed to control himself as he calmly spoke. "Eva, I'm sure you're capable. And I know you've probably done it before. But I would really like to help. So I would appreciate it if you would just let someone help you and let me drive down the mountain."

Eva could hardly breathe as she stared at him. Was that true? Did she not know how to let people help her? And how did he know that when she barely knew anything about him?

Still, she felt herself reach into her pocket, take out the keys, and hand them to him in perfect silence.

"Thank you." He smiled.

She felt like she had been hoodwinked, as she watched him climb into the driver's seat of the pickup truck. But she turned and walked around to the other side and climbed into the passenger seat. She hoped she wouldn't regret this.

He cranked the truck and carefully adjusted everything from the seat, to the mirrors, and the volume on the radio. Christmas music quietly streamed through the car and he checked behind and then pulled out of the garage.

"And we're off," Eva said.

"Looks like it," Logan said. He fell silent then and kept his eyes on the road without wavering.

Eva tapped her fingers on the arm rest as they crawled along at what felt like a snail's pace. She knew he was being cautious, but she also wanted to get back before Christmas was over. She debated whether to talk to him. He seemed to have all his focus on the road as they began their climb down the mountain. But after several minutes she couldn't take it anymore. Mountains be darned. "So does your family always take a trip for Christmas?"

"No," he said without looking at her.

"No, not always, or no, not usually?" She tried to lead him into saying more.

"No, never," he said. "This is our first trip together as a family in quite a long time."

"Really?" She raised her eyebrows in surprise. "Well, I'm honored that you chose my little inn for your first family trip in quite a long time."

He let out a sigh and he turned a corner to the right. "Actually, if I'm being honest, I didn't really want to come."

Eva was surprised at how she felt hurt by that. But he continued.

"Not because I didn't want to come here. I just didn't really want to do a trip at all. And Christmas, well, it just isn't really our thing."

"Thing?" She practically yelled. "How can Christmas not be your thing? It's the best thing ever!"

He shrugged. "It was fun as a kid. But when my brother and I got older, it just became less important, I guess. We still get together on the twenty-fifth, but it's more like a one day and it's over kind of thing." His voice dropped as he said, "And it's not the happiest day."

"But there are presents, right?"

"Um, sure." He cleared his throat, and it seemed like he almost said more, but he stopped himself. "It's just a day. Not usually a two-week vacation together kind of holiday."

Eva gave a little humph. "If I could spend two weeks on vacation with my family, I would have zero complaints about it."

He quickly glanced at her and then gave his attention right back to the road. "Do you mean your whole family? Or your grandparents?"

Eva clamped her mouth shut. Why would he ask her that? She cleared her throat to push away the emotion the question brought. "Well, I guess it would be my grandparents, if they were still here. But they were really the only family I had."

He paused as if he was afraid to ask.

She didn't wait and told him what she knew he wanted to know. "My parents didn't want me."

He gently pressed the brakes until they came to a slow stop. He glanced behind to see that there was a clear stretch of road with no one coming. "Eva, I'm sorry. I didn't mean to ask about something so personal. You didn't have to tell me that. But I'm also sorry that that happened to you."

His kindness brought tears to her eyes. Tears she hadn't

let fall in a very, very long time. "It's all right," she said, waving a hand in the air. "It was their choice, and it's not exactly a secret. My parents got married in college, they were both very young. They didn't really plan to have me... or any kids, I guess. At least not while they were in college. My dad thought having a kid at that age would slow him down, keep them from living their own life, and from being successful in his career. He told my mom he didn't want that. And he left her."

Eva watched as Logan's expression hardened. But he remained silent.

"My mom came home to my grandparents and stayed there until I was born. She lived there with me until I was about six months old. Then she drove off one night and left a note saying she was going home to my dad and she was sorry, but she wasn't ready to be a mom." Eva shrugged. "I guess she was never ready."

"You've never met her?" Logan asked.

Eva shook her head. "Not her, or my dad. My grandparents are the only parents I ever knew."

"I'm sorry, Eva. You deserve better than that."

Eva stared into his eyes as he spoke those words. She could have melted into them. But she steeled herself against the emotion and gave a little laugh. "But listen to me, just talking your ears off. Let's get going."

Logan was quiet again, and Eva wondered if she had shared too much. She didn't know much about him, but she had figured out he was pretty private, and telling him her sob story of a life was probably way too much information.

10

*L*ogan had never felt so disappointed and angry at two people he had never met. How could anyone not want a baby? Their own flesh and blood? Just to go off and have a life where they didn't have to care for someone else. And poor Eva, who had never had her parents in her life. It made him hurt for her.

But now in the quietness, he also felt like she had entrusted him with her story. He hoped he was worthy of that trust. He knew all too well that letting people into your life made you vulnerable. But Eva seemed open and honest, like she had nothing to hide. It almost made him want to tell her more about himself. But he had to be careful. There was too much on the line for him to be an open book.

Still, maybe he could share something, just so she knew that it meant a lot to him that she had told him about her parents.

"Thanks for letting me drive today. I, uh, I don't really like riding with other people driving."

"Oh?" Eva said. "Are you a control freak or something?"

He bristled at those words that he had heard before. "No, I don't think so, anyway. But I was in a car accident once in the passenger seat. It wasn't like this where it was snowy with ice on the roads, it was a perfectly fine day, and should have been a normal drive. But the driver just wasn't paying attention. He was eating food and texting on his phone, and he didn't look up in time. I will never forget the feeling of stomping my foot on the floor as if I could press the brakes, but of course that didn't help. I yelled for him to stop, but it was too late. We crashed into the car in front of us that was stopped at a red light. It pushed us and that car into the intersection and we were hit by a car coming from the other direction."

Eva gasped and pressed her palm to her chest. "Oh my, I'm so sorry. I'm glad you were okay, though."

Logan cleared his throat. "I wasn't for a while. My arm was broken and I had to have pins put in my ankle from where it was crushed."

"Logan," Eva whispered. "I'm so sorry."

"I'm all right," he said. "But I prefer to drive whenever I'm in a vehicle."

"I can imagine why."

"But also, I really did want to help you today. You know, you've really been handling this whole snowstorm remarkably well. I would have guessed you had a lot of experience and training and not that you've only been running the inn for a short time."

"Thanks," Eva beamed with the praise.

"But I also know it has to be a lot to handle by yourself." Logan knew what it was like to be the top man in charge. "So if I can help take a little bit of the load off, I'm happy to do it."

"But you really shouldn't have to. You're a guest, after all. It's my job to take care of my guests."

"Yes, but I guess it's actually nice to help out when it's not my job."

Silence fell between them for a few minutes. Silence was comfortable for Logan, but he could tell Eva was squirming in her seat.

Finally it was too much for her and she asked her next question as if it burst out of her. "Are you still friends with him?"

Logan turned to look at her. "Who?" he asked.

"The guy who was driving the car?"

As if a dark cloud passed over his soul, Logan felt the darkness come over him. "Well, I guess you could say so. He's not someone I can push out of my life completely. But we're not on great terms."

Eva's voice dropped when she said, "It's your brother, isn't it?"

Logan almost stopped the car. "How did you know?"

Eva gave him a kind smile. "It's a little hard to ignore how you guys are around each other. It's a little... tense."

Logan sighed. "That's a nice way to put it. But you're right." He might as well tell her now, since she figured it out on her own. Maybe he wasn't doing as good of a job of hiding things as he thought. "It was five years ago, on Christmas Eve. Jordan had waited until the last minute to buy Mom and Dad Christmas gifts. He convinced me to go to the store with him to find something for them. I didn't want to at first, but I also wanted them to have nice presents from him, and I didn't trust him to pick something out. He can be so irresponsible sometimes." Logan ran a hand over his head. "But he was excited to buy them something. He did always like giving gifts, just didn't think far enough ahead about buying them. But then the accident happened. So there were no presents and my parents spent Christmas in the hospital."

"Was Jordan hurt too?"

Logan nodded. "He hit his head on the window, so they were monitoring him for a concussion. But his side wasn't hit, so he was all right other than that and a few bruises." Logan swallowed hard to push down the emotions. "I don't remember much about those few days. But I know that Mom was a wreck. She insisted I come back to her house when I got out of the hospital to recover. When I got there, all the Christmas decorations were gone. Since then, we've had very low key Christmas celebrations. And we don't swap gifts anymore. It's almost as if Mom thinks it's her fault. So she stopped making a big deal about it."

"That's sad," Eva said. "Christmas should be fun and special. She shouldn't feel guilty about wanting that with her family."

"I know," Logan said. "That's why we're here. I would have been fine with moving right along and showing up for Christmas day for lunch and no presents. But Mom wanted this trip." He shrugged. "I feel like she deserves something nice."

Eva gave him a look that he didn't quite understand. But they had made it safely down the mountain and stopped at a stop light in the middle of town. She pointed the way to the store and he turned, following her directions.

He pulled into a parking spot and put the truck in park. He let out a big breath, relieved that they had arrived safely. At least they were halfway done with the driving.

Eva jumped down from the truck and ran around to his side. "I want to try to be as quick as possible. So I have a list." She shot her arm up into the air, but just as she did, she stepped on a patch of ice in the parking lot. Her feet slipped and she let out a yelp.

Logan moved fast and caught her arm. It was enough to balance her and keep her from ending up flat on her back on the asphalt. "Thanks," she said, meeting his eyes. She held his gaze for just a moment before she let out a laugh. "That could have been really embarrassing."

He laughed too, and the sound surprised him. She took quick steps towards the store, breaking the grip he had on her arm. He watched her for a few seconds. She had on a thick coat and he wore gloves, but despite that, the sensation of touching her arm had shot through his body, shocking him and freezing him in this spot. He gave his head a shake to get himself moving and followed her in the store.

Eva acted as if she was a contestant on a grocery shopping game show, whizzing back and forth from one side of the aisle to the other. Logan could appreciate how she had mapped out her list in the order of the store, so there was no backtracking or forgetting an item on an aisle. She had wanted to be quick, and she got her wish. In what Logan thought must be some kind of record-breaking time, they headed back to the truck with two grocery carts full of food and supplies.

"Are you sure we got enough coffee?" he asked, his eyes twinkling.

Eva laughed. "I stopped short of emptying the entire shelf into the cart. I figured we should leave some for other people. But yes, I think we got enough. I sure hope so, anyway. I think we're doing pretty good, but I'd like to avoid making this trip again soon."

Logan had begun loading bags into the back of the truck, but he paused to look at her. "What? You don't like riding to town with me?"

"Oh no, I like that part." Eva seemed to hear her own words as they came out and her eyes went wide. "I mean, I'm glad I didn't have to come alone." She cleared her throat. "You've been good company."

Logan grinned. He had to admit that he'd enjoyed the

time so far. "You too," he said. Before he could let himself think anymore, he handed her a bag, "But let's get back soon."

11

*E*va had thought about riding to town with Logan the rest of the day. She had been worried it would be awkward, or worse, silent. But it had been fine. Good even. Dare she say it? Great. He had been the perfect gentleman, following her through the store and lifting the heavy items. And taking charge to drive them safely down the mountain and back up. She couldn't remember when anyone had done something like that for her.

She had always felt safest with her grandparents. And her grandmother had always looked to her grandfather to be the head of the house. Eva had wondered what that was like for her and wondered if her grandmother ever wanted to shout out her opinion or just grab the car keys and tell him where they were going.

It had been hard for Eva to imagine being a subdued, quiet housewife. She had plans and goals, and she liked being in charge.

So normally, it would have bothered her for someone to tell her they were going to drive. Especially a man. But with

Logan, he was so nice about it. Not demanding or bossing her around, just giving her the option to take a load off.

Was that what it would be like to be in a relationship? A good relationship? She wouldn't know. She had pushed off most guys who were interested in her in college. And before that, her grandfather had scared away any guy who looked at her in high school. Sure, she'd been on a few dates, but not enough to call it a relationship. Besides, she knew too well that people could leave you behind for better opportunities. And she wasn't planning to open herself up to that kind of hurt again.

Now that the inn was quiet and all the guests were asleep, she walked through the downstairs, just checking on everything. She had filled the pantry that afternoon and in her excitement, she might have had a little too much coffee. Now she knew she would be awake for a while. But she didn't mind. She loved her guests, but she enjoyed the quiet of her own inn without anyone else around.

When she reached the bottom of the stairs, she noticed a light on in the kitchen. That wasn't unusual, they often kept a light on in case anyone came downstairs. She didn't think anything of it. She turned the corner and switched on the kitchen light. "Oh!" Her hand flew to her chest, and she immediately turned the light back off when she saw someone sitting at the kitchen counter. "Sorry, I didn't hear anyone in here. Logan?" She asked as her eyes adjusted to the dim light.

"I guess you caught me." He held up the container with chocolate chip cookies.

"What?" Eva's eyes grew wide. "I didn't think there were any of those left!"

A guilty look crossed his face. "Well, I might have put some away for safekeeping."

Eva tried to give him a stern look, but it was too late, she was already laughing. "You didn't take them to your room?"

He shook his head. "How would I eat them there with no milk?"

"Good point."

"But since you caught me red-handed, I guess I'll have to share them."

She nodded with her best serious face. "Yes, that is the punishment for hiding the last of the cookies."

Logan held out the container to her.

"I have to get milk first."

"Of course," he said. Then he placed the cookies on the counter in front of the stool next to him.

Eva glanced at him as she found a coffee mug and filled it with milk. She considered for a moment whether to stay on this side of the counter, or take the seat next to him. Sitting next to him sounded nice. But so did looking at him from this side of the counter. She told herself to stop thinking and do the natural thing. And that apparently was to sit beside him, since her feet carried her there.

"So what's keeping you up?" Eva asked.

Logan turned to look at her and tilted his chin. "Just can't sleep, I guess."

"Did you have as much coffee as I did this afternoon?"

He laughed then, and the sound did something funny to her heart. "No, I don't think anyone had as much coffee as you did."

Eva held her coffee mug in the air. "True. I'm probably the champion coffee drinker today."

"So that's why you can't sleep?" he asked.

"I guess so. But I also like to check things out after everyone is asleep. You know, make sure there aren't any chocolate chip cookie thieves lurking around." She nudged him with her elbow.

He nudged her back. "I guess you can't be too careful."

"Do you usually have a hard time sleeping?" She asked.

He shrugged. "Sometimes. Business keeps me busy, I guess, so my mind is always working."

"But you're on vacation. You're not supposed to be worried about business right now."

"I know. I guess that's the curse of being the boss."

"The boss?" Eva leaned away from him with wide-eyes. "You didn't tell me you were a boss."

"Oh, um. Did I not?"

Eva saw a look of almost panic in his eyes. "No, you didn't. Why? Is it a secret?"

He cleared his throat. "Not a secret. I guess I just don't go around saying I'm the boss." He paused and rolled his eyes to the ceiling. "Except for just now when I guess I did."

Eva chuckled. "Well, no matter. I'm the boss too. Nobody tells me what to do."

"I can see that," he said.

"Hey now, just because I'm the boss doesn't mean I'm bossy."

He held up his hands. "I didn't say you were."

"Well, I'm not. All my employees like working here and say I'm a good boss."

Logan nodded slowly. "I believe you." He met her eyes then, and Eva wondered how long she could stare at him. His eyes were kind and fun, but also held a mystery, what kind of mystery she didn't know. She sure would like to find out.

"Well, you know what Bing Crosby says you should do if you can't sleep."

He furrowed his eyebrows. "What?"

"Oh, come on," she gave him a playful hit on his arm. "From 'White Christmas'?"

"Remember I'm not the Christmas movie buff."

"Oh right, that's me." She grinned. "He says you should fall asleep counting your blessings."

"Is that so?"

"Mmhmm." Eva pressed her lips together as she nodded. She sure would like to count Logan as one of her blessings. An idea came to her and she jumped up off the stool. "Hey, I know. I've had enough coffee to last awhile, and you can't sleep. So the only thing to do is start getting you educated in Christmas movies."

"Really?" He scrunched his nose and tilted his head. "Is that the only thing to do?"

"It's the perfect thing to do! Come on." She grabbed his arm and began pulling him into the living room. When she walked by the couch, she let go and pointed for him to sit. Then she went to the shelf and ran her finger across the titles as she looked for her favorite. "Aha! We're in luck. No one has borrowed 'White Christmas', so we can start with that." Without waiting for him to agree, she ran to the DVD player and put in the movie.

"Lucky indeed," Logan said.

She humphed and walked over to stand in front of him. She crossed her arms and stared at him. "Are you really going to be such a Scrooge?"

"That's the wrong Christmas movie," he said.

"But really, are you going to hate watching it that much?"

Logan looked at her for a minute, as if considering his answer. Then he slowly reached up and took hold of her arms and uncrossed them. He pulled her hands until she sat down beside him. "Actually, I think I won't mind at all if I'm watching it with you."

Eva was glad for the dim lights in the room as she felt her face flush as red as the lights on the Christmas tree. For once she had nothing to say. So instead, she reached for the remote and turned on the movie. She settled back in her seat as the opening credits began to roll. And she didn't hate it that Logan's shoulder touched hers as Bing Crosby began to sing.

✳

EVA'S COFFEE MUST HAVE WORN OFF SOMEWHERE AROUND THE fourth musical number in the movie. Logan felt her head fall onto his shoulder. He jerked his head in surprise and realized that her eyes were closed and her breathing was slow and deep. How could she fall asleep when he was just beginning to enjoy the movie? He guessed Bing Crosby had lulled her to sleep with his song about counting your blessings.

Logan thought this moment was climbing up on that list.

He hadn't taken much time lately to think about his blessings. He was too busy being the responsible member of the family and running the publishing company. Sure, each magazine had its own staff, and passed decisions up the chain. But he still had a lot of things to take care of and responsibilities to handle.

But there were blessings too. Like knowing he was getting up every day to go to work for a company that he loved. Not only because it had been in his family for generations, all the way from a small newspaper in a North Carolina town the size of Mayberry to the publishing giant it had become. But because it was work he was proud to do. In a time where some companies were downsizing and cutting back on production, they had forged on. And Logan was proud of the company and their employees.

His family was a blessing too. His parents had always supported him and had tried their best not to spoil him, even though that would have been easy to do. But how had he ended up being the non-spoiled brother, while Jordan was happy to sit around and enjoy his family's wealth?

If Logan had a nickel for every time Jordan was late to work, or never showed up at all... well maybe he did. But it was a lot. Why couldn't he care about the company? Or his job? Or anything, for that matter? And then he shows up on

BILLIONAIRE AT THE CHRISTMAS INN | 61

this trip with his parents, and Logan had barely seen his brother. Even after his mother made them agree to stop hiding in their rooms. Logan was pretty sure Jordan had a video game system he was playing up there.

He sighed. Being angry with his brother wasn't going to make him enjoy Christmas right now, so he decided to stop thinking about it.

Eva took a deep breath and let it out. Then she slowly lifted her head and turned to face Logan. Her eyes grew wide and she must have realized she fell asleep on his shoulder. "Oh, how long have I been out?"

"Not long, I don't think. Maybe a song or two?"

She sat up and stretched as a grin spread over her face. "You're counting time in songs now?"

"It seemed appropriate."

"Are you a Christmas movie convert now?"

"Hmm." He let his arm fall across the back of the couch before she leaned back. "I don't know. I might need two or three more movies before I decide."

Eva smiled. "I have the perfect ones in mind. But it might have to be tomorrow night." She covered a yawn.

"Sure. I'm free tomorrow night. If you are."

"Are you asking me to watch a movie with you?"

Logan's smile grew wide. "Actually, I think you asked me."

"Did I?" She tapped her chin with her index finger. "Hmm. I'm too tired to remember. But if you're asking, or if I'm asking. My answer is yes."

Logan felt his heart skip a beat. "Mine is too."

*L*ogan stared out the window of his room, sipping a cup of coffee. He had brought it back up, along with a plate from breakfast. There were a lot of people down there and he just needed some time to himself.

But what he really needed was time to think about Eva. What was it about her that made him want to open up to her? She made him feel comfortable in a way he hadn't in a long time. That was what scared him. He had promised himself he wouldn't let anyone in unless he knew for sure he could trust them. And since there was never a way to be sure, that just meant he stayed closed off.

He had learned his lesson. More than once. Being in his position with his family's company and family money had brought out the worst in some people. But they didn't show it as their worst. They showed it by being nice and friendly and making sure to become part of his life. But every time he thought maybe he had found someone who actually cared about him, he would find out that they only wanted his money. Usually too late.

But not now.

Did that mean he could trust Eva? She didn't know about his family or the money.

"Ugh," he let out the groan as he crashed on the couch. That also meant she didn't really know who he was. He couldn't deny that he had feelings for her, and he thought maybe she liked him too. But how could she? Would she feel the same if she knew the truth? Or would it give her an opportunity to try to get to him for his money?

Logan stared at the ceiling, it didn't look old, at least not as old as he knew the inn was. Eva must have sunk a lot of money into this place. Would she want him to help her pay for more renovations if she knew the resources he had?

A knock at his door startled him. He went to the door, and for just a moment he let himself hope it was Eva at the door. He put on a smile and opened it.

His smile faded when he saw his brother standing in front of him.

"Hey," Jordan said. "Can I come in?"

Logan stepped back to allow him to enter, but he didn't say anything.

Jordan made his way into the room and took a quick glance around before making himself comfortable on the couch. "What do you think of this place, anyway? Kind of cooky, isn't it? Only Mom would pick an inn with rooms named after Christmas movies."

"What do you want, Jordan?"

Jordan snapped his head around to look at Logan. "What? I can't come to my own brother's room to hang out and shoot the breeze?"

"Sure you can. But I don't think you did." Logan leveled his gaze as he took a seat opposite Jordan in the chair.

"Fine. I'll get to the point." Jordan sat up and linked his fingers together in front of him. "I want out."

Immediately anger rushed through Logan's body. He felt

certain he knew what his brother meant, but still he asked. "What do you mean, out?"

"Out of the business."

Logan blew out a puff of air and stood to pace the room. "You've got to be kidding me. This is a joke right?"

"Not a joke. I'm serious. I want out."

"How can you say that?" Logan heard his voice echoing against the walls and told himself to calm down. "You barely show up for work, you're late when you do, you do almost nothing and you still sit around in your expensive apartment or travel on the private jet. What do you think you're going to do?"

Jordan's own anger flashed across his face. "I guess that's my business, isn't it?"

"It's my business too. Our family has worked hard for generations to have what we have."

"Yeah, yeah. I know, I've heard it all, okay? Our family, the great Bradford family," he held up his hands and motioned air quotes. "That's all I've heard my entire life, and I'm over it. I don't want it anymore. And I want out." He stood then and faced Logan. "I want out and I don't have to explain it to you." He paused and took several breaths. "I thought maybe I would. I thought maybe you would understand and you could help me talk to Mom and Dad. But I was crazy for thinking that, even for a second. You're Bradford born and raised and you can't see past that for anything."

"I'm who Mom and Dad raised me to be. And who our grandparents raised our Dad to be. I thought they raised you the same, but something must have gone wrong, because we couldn't be more different."

Jordan huffed. "You're right. Sorry I thought I could depend on my brother. I guess we'll never see eye to eye on me living my own life. Have fun living the life everyone else always planned for you." With that, he turned and walked out the door and slammed it behind him.

Logan watched him go and picked up a throw pillow and threw it in the direction Jordan had walked. That was as violent as he would get with his brother. He stared at the red and white snowflake pillow with the tassels on the corners and it almost made him laugh. But the moment didn't call for that. It was a picture though of life with Jordan. Jordan did what he wanted, pitched fits, and stomped out of rooms. But did he ever pay any consequences? No, he was a fluffy throw pillow that everybody tiptoed around so they wouldn't hurt his feelings.

Logan crashed onto the couch and stared again at the ceiling. It was the same place he had been before his brother came in, but his thoughts had changed.

No, he couldn't trust anyone. He couldn't even trust his own brother to continue the family legacy. How could he possibly trust a girl he just met and shared Christmas cookies with? That would just set him up for disappointment again. And he didn't want to watch anyone else walk out of his life.

13

That evening Christmas music filled the inn as it played through the surround sound speakers. Eva knew they were bought by her grandfather many years ago, and they weren't state-of-the art, but they were sure doing their job tonight. Guests sipped hot cocoa and holiday punch and danced around the room to Christmas favorites.

Eva smiled, watching them. This was exactly what she had hoped for. Her guests were relaxing and enjoying the holiday. But she couldn't help but notice that one guest in particular was missing. She fiddled with the pearl necklace she wore, a gift left to her by her grandmother. She had checked her outfit in the mirror too many times before she came downstairs. The red sweater with a black skirt and tights seemed fitting for Christmas Eve. But she would be lying if she told herself she hadn't wondered what Logan would think. And now he wasn't even here. She glanced at Vickie across the room. The woman smiled and held her glass of punch up in the air. But she too looked around the room and then back at Eva. She shrugged and then pointed towards the stairs.

Eva followed where she pointed and then looked back to Vickie. Vickie nodded and Eva blushed, understanding her message. She took a deep breath, tugged on her sweater and made her way up the stairs. When she knocked on Logan's door, she was surprised at how fast he opened it.

"Oh, hey," His expression had been tense, maybe even angry, but it softened when he looked at her.

"Hey," Eva said. "You know you're missing a pretty good party downstairs."

He crossed his arms and leaned against the doorframe. Boy, did he look good in that black sweater, despite the fact that black practically said "Bah humbug" this evening. "Oh, am I?"

Eva met his eyes and wanted to let herself get lost in his gaze. "Mmhmm," she said.

"I was just getting ready to come down."

"Oh, my bad." Eva started to step backwards.

"Don't be," he said, reaching for her arm. He held both of her arms in his hands for a moment. "I just need to grab something. Would you like to come in and wait for me?"

Eva hesitated only for a moment. "Sure," she heard herself say. She never would have imagined that she would walk into a guest's room for any reason other than extra towels or to pick up a food tray. But here she was. She stepped in and her black heels clicked across the hardwood floor. Logan walked in front of her, but turned around and his eyes roamed over her as he took her in.

"You look nice," he said.

"Thanks." Eva fingered her necklace again, suddenly feeling very nervous.

Logan took two steps closer to her. "No, like really nice." He reached for her hand and pulled it away from her necklace. "Are you all right? I'm sorry, are you uncomfortable?"

She gave a half-hearted laugh, trying to prove that she

wasn't. "No, I'm fine. But I'm not used to just walking into a room where a guest is staying."

He kept her hand in his and her heart pounded at a volume that rivaled the music downstairs. "Do you think of me as just another guest?" Logan asked, still moving closer.

Her eyes flickered up to his. "Well, I'm starting not to."

For a moment she felt like the world around her moved in slow motion and she moved without thinking. As Logan came close, he pulled her into his arms. She could smell his cologne and she breathed it in, telling herself to memorize this moment. He looked into her eyes and they seemed to breathe in unison, as if there was nothing else in the room. Logan's eyes flicked down to her mouth and back up to her eyes. Just as he began to lean in, a knock sounded at the door.

Logan dropped his arms so fast Eva almost fell backwards. She righted herself and turned to the door as Logan said, "Come in."

"There you are." Jordan's voice sounded enthusiastic. "Mom wants us to get a family picture tonight. She told me to tell you."

"When?"

"Tonight, I just said tonight." Jordan's eyes flashed with frustration.

"I mean, when did she ask you to tell me that?"

Jordan threw his hands up in the air. "I don't know. Yesterday, maybe."

"So you're telling me now?"

"Look, she asked me to tell you. I told you." Jordan walked out the way he came and slammed the door.

Logan forced his fingers through his hair as he turned back from the door and let out a huff.

"What's going on there?" Eva asked. Still reeling from the moment before the interruption.

Logan held a hand out towards the closed door. "That's just Jordan."

Eva pursed her lips and tucked a strand of hair behind her ear. "Yeah. I've seen that since you got here. But it seems like it's reached a new level."

Logan turned to face her and seemed to weigh his choices. Was he going to tell her or leave her in the dark? It took him too long to ponder it, and she turned towards the door. "It's fine if you don't want to tell me. It's not my business."

Logan caught her hand and kept her from reaching for the door knob. "I do want to tell you. It's just complicated."

She turned to face him and tried to take her hand back, but he held it firmly. "Complicated doesn't bother me. But if you don't want to tell me, I can go back to hosting my party."

Logan sighed. "My parents don't know yet, but Jordan is making decisions. He wants to leave his job and do who knows what. He's always been like this, so I guess the decision has been a long time coming. But it's still the wrong decision. And it's going to hurt my parents."

"And hurt you, too?"

Logan's eyes were sad as he looked at her. "He hurt me a long time ago. I've done my best to not let it affect me."

Eva reached up and touched his face. "But it always hurts when family disappoints us."

"Yes. I guess it does."

"Is there anything you can do about his decision?"

Logan shook his head. "I don't think so. I've tried before, but he's made up his mind."

"Then let's not worry about it now. It's Christmas Eve, let's enjoy it."

Logan gave her half a smile. "I'll try."

"Oh, come on, you can do better than that."

He laughed. "All right. Let's go have fun."

Eva squeezed his hand and then let go as she turned and opened the door.

Logan seemed to lighten up as they made their way down the stairs, and he smiled for his mom when she greeted him with a hug. When she let him go, she turned and hugged Eva too. Eva took a sharp breath as Vickie enveloped her. How long had it been since she had been hugged like that?

When Vickie released her, Eva took in the room. The Christmas music, the lights of the tree glowing, the room full of happy people. This was everything she could have asked for her first Christmas as the owner of the inn.

Her gaze turned to Logan and she wondered if she dared wish for anything more.

A commotion sounded from the direction of the kitchen, and one of the guests came dancing through with a bunch of mistletoe on a long candy cane stick. Eva's eyes grew wide as the woman held the mistletoe over each couple and the guests around them began to chant. "Mistletoe, mistletoe, kiss, kiss!" The couples happily obliged.

Vickie lit up when the mistletoe hung over her head and she reached for Robert's hands and laid a generous smooch on his lips. Without missing a beat, Vickie pointed at Eva.

Eva's eyes rolled above her and she heard the guests chanting for her. Vickie reached out and gave Logan a push until he was standing right beside Eva.

Her heart pounded and the sounds of the Christmas music seemed to dim as she looked up at Logan. Would he really do it? Eva sucked in a breath as their eyes met. He stepped close and she tipped her chin up to him. He tilted his head down to hers and just as he neared her, he blinked. Then he shook his head and stepped back.

"Aww, come on!" Cried the guest with the mistletoe.

The sound brought Eva back to the realization that she was standing in her inn with all her guests, and she had almost made a huge mistake. She felt her cheeks burn red and she didn't meet Logan's eyes as she pretended to laugh it off. The mistletoe moved on to new victims and Eva excused herself, saying she should check on things in the kitchen.

What was she thinking? Of course, he didn't want to actually be with her. For him it's just a vacation, and she was just a fling for fun. But he wasn't about to kiss her in front of everyone and make a fool of himself. She opened a few cabinets, as if there was something to check on, then slammed each of them back.

"Did the cabinets hurt your feelings too?" Logan's voice was right behind her. She didn't move, her hands fell to the counter and she held on as if it were her life raft. "Or am I the only one doing that today?" Tears burned her eyes and threatened to fall as she realized how right he was. "Eva," he whispered. The hurt in his voice made her turn to see his face. His expression matched his tone, and despite her own hurt, she wanted to make it go away. "I'm sorry," he said.

She waved a hand in the air. "It's fine. You don't have to do anything you don't want to. I know, I'm just the girl running the inn where you happen to be vacationing. You're probably right, you don't want to make a mistake that will always be a Christmas memory."

Logan reached for her then. He took her face in his hands and locked eyes with her. "You're wrong. I didn't back away because I didn't want to. You're right that it felt like it would be a mistake. But not for the reason you think. You may have noticed that I'm a pretty private person. I don't like the whole world to know about my life."

"Yeah, I've noticed. You keep things pretty close to the vest."

"So I don't want to kiss you in front of my whole family, and a room full of people I don't even know."

"You don't?"

He shook his head slowly. "No, I don't. And I don't think it will be a memory that I regret. But I wanted it to be the right memory. A memory I could hold on to forever."

"What?"

"This," he said, just before he closed the distance between them. His lips met hers and Eva let out a soft sigh. She lifted her hands to his chest, gripping his sweater. He held her face, gently but firmly as he kissed her.

Logan pulled back and looked her in the eyes. Eva kept her grip on him as she slowly opened her eyes. She searched for the right words to say, but the only right thing seemed to be to kiss him again. So she did. All the magic of Christmas seemed to pour into it. It was like Christmas morning, hot cocoa and a fire, and twinkling lights all bundled up together. Eva felt warm from her fingertips to her toes. She had never felt such a sense of belonging as Logan wrapped his arms around her and deepened the kiss.

When he pulled back this time, they were both breathless. "That was a memory I'll hang on to," Eva said.

Logan smiled and he looked different than he had before. It was as if he'd been holding something back, but now he looked free and happy. "I kind of hate to share you, but do you think we should get back to the party?" He slipped his hand into hers.

Eva stood up on her tiptoes and kissed him once more, then she nodded. "I don't want to miss out on the celebration."

14

*L*ogan couldn't remember when he had been this excited about Christmas morning. He woke up with a smile on his face and he had no doubt it would stay there all day. Even Jordan couldn't bug him today. He was up and dressed and crept down the stairs before anyone else was awake. He was afraid Eva would have beaten him to it, but he had even managed to be earlier than her.

Not for long, though. He had only been in the kitchen long enough to find the coffee and get the coffee maker going before she padded through the entryway. Her eyes grew wide when she saw him. "What are you doing?" She whispered.

"Making you coffee," he whispered back. He stepped back until he was leaning against the counter. "Merry Christmas."

"Merry Christmas," she said, coming to stand in front of him. Her smile spread wide.

Logan couldn't resist her. "Come here." He reached out and took her in his arms. His lips found hers, giving her a proper Christmas morning greeting. When they parted, he kept his arms around her and pressed his nose against hers.

"I didn't get you a present. You know the snow and all. So I thought I could at least make you coffee to start the day off right."

"Well, that just might be my favorite Christmas present ever." Eva smiled.

Logan laughed. "You're easy to please."

"Yep, just keep me caffeinated."

"That's easy enough."

"What about you? If you could have anything you wanted for Christmas, what would it be?

He wondered if he should tell her that, in fact, he could have anything he wanted for Christmas. But decided that was a serious discussion for a later time. "I can honestly say, this Christmas, I want nothing more than to be here, snowed in with you."

Eva's eyes twinkled with the laughter behind them. "That's good, since you don't have a choice."

"What would a Christmas morning look like for you, normally?"

Eva smiled a sad sort of smile. "This is pretty normal for me. There were always people at the inn, so my grandparents would take care of the guests. But we always had a special time as a family. I would sneak into their room as early as I could, usually as soon as the sun was up. My grandmother would come down and make me a cup of hot chocolate and we would snuggle up around the tree they had in their room. My grandfather would read the Christmas story from the Bible and then we would get to open presents." She stopped and smiled. "They were the best at presents. It wasn't always the biggest things, or the most expensive, but they put a lot of thought into it, so the gifts were always special."

"What was your favorite gift?"

"The year my grandmother gave me a sewing machine."

"Really?" Logan loved watching the way she lit up as she told a story.

"Yeah. But it wasn't just the gift. My grandmother spent months teaching me how to sew. We made outfits and doll clothes and a couple of quilts."

"Do you still sew?"

She shook her head. "Not really. I know how, but it's been a long time. And I never really did a project without her standing over my shoulder. It would seem strange to do it without her."

Logan nodded.

"What about you? What's your favorite Christmas gift?"

He blew out a breath to give himself a minute to think about his answer. True, he had had plenty of big presents, and expensive ones, including a trip to Hawaii when he was twelve and a car when he was sixteen. But he knew what the real answer was. "It seems simple, but I'd have to say the year I got a bike for Christmas."

"Oh, that's a good gift."

"It was. It's like your sewing machine. I remember my dad taking me out in the driveway in my pajamas that same day and teaching me to ride." He rubbed the back of his head and laughed. "I had bumps and bruises to show for it, but by the end of the day I was riding. That was a good Christmas."

Eva bit her lip like she did when she wanted to say something but wasn't sure if she should. Logan was getting used to that look. "Go ahead," he said. "Ask."

"Did Jordan get a bike too?"

Logan's heart thudded at the mention of his brother. He was trying hard not to think about him this morning. He nodded. "Yes, he did. We both learned to ride that day."

"I just wondered."

Logan tilted his head. "Why do you wonder about me and my brother so much?"

Eva shrugged. "I don't know. I don't have any siblings, and I just hate to see the two of you at odds with each other. I wondered if it's always been that way."

"No. And yes. We got along as kids, we played a lot together and did a lot of the same things. But I guess I was always hard on him as a big brother, and he has always liked to give me grief about it."

Eva tapped her chin with her index finger. "So, do you think you're too hard on him?"

Logan sighed. This was not the conversation he wanted to be having right now. "I guess I am at times. But it's only because I want him to grow up and take responsibility for his own life."

"Hmm." Eva said.

"What?"

"Nothing. I just wonder if maybe he is grown up, but it's hard to see because you're his big brother. And maybe just because he doesn't want the same things as you, doesn't mean he's not taking responsibility."

Logan felt himself take a step back in his mind. "I haven't really thought about it that way." He wanted to be upset and if it were anyone else, he would tell them they were wrong. But Eva was so cute when she said it, and he could tell she was really thinking hard about his relationship with his brother. So maybe he could think about that. He kissed her on the nose. "I'll try to think about that."

She gave him a pointed look. "And you'll play nice today?"

He held his hand up. "Promise. Scouts' honor."

"Maybe the two of you will make a truce, it can be a Christmas miracle."

Logan laughed. He knew it would take an actual miracle. But maybe with Eva, anything was possible.

15

*E*va smiled at the faces around the living room. It had been a full morning already and she hoped it would last all day. Or maybe forever. She'd be happy either way. Several of the guests had come down and enjoyed coffee. Eva had given Joyce the day off, but she had prepared french toast casseroles the night before that Eva popped in the oven, and fruit trays to set out. Eva had been able to sit and enjoy breakfast. Most everyone headed out to enjoy the snow, or back to their rooms to open presents in private. But Logan's family gathered around the living room. Logan tugged on Eva's hand and walked her into the living room to join them.

Vickie gave a quiet gasp when she saw the two of them holding hands, but her smile was so big, Eva thought it might break.

Now she sat next to Logan on the couch. Vickie and Robert sat in chairs near the fireplace, and Jordan sprawled out on the floor. True to his word, Logan had been cordial to his brother, and now the family was sharing stories from their childhood.

"Remember when you pushed me out of that tree?" Jordan asked Logan.

"I didn't you, you jumped," Logan said.

"Right, I climbed thirty feet up in a tree and jumped out face first."

Logan shrugged. "You always were a daredevil."

"Whether you jumped or were pushed, it turned into an expensive adventure."

Jordan grinned as he explained to Eva. "I broke my arm. And I insisted I couldn't get up off the ground, so they had to call an ambulance to take me to the hospital."

"That's right," Vickie said. "And I had to bribe you with ice cream and balloons and a new game for your video system to get you to hold your arm out for the x-ray."

"It hurt really bad."

"I'm sure it did." Vickie patted his shoulder. "And what about you? Logan, I seem to remember bribing you some too."

"Yes, but that's different. You weren't bribing me to be seen by a doctor."

"No, I was bribing you to take music lessons."

"Music lessons?" Eva's eyebrows shot up as she turned to him. "You play an instrument?"

"No, no," Logan held up his hands.

"Yes, he does. A few, actually. But piano is his best by far."

"When were you going to tell me you play piano?" Eva punched him in the arm. "I have a perfectly good piano here, and no one to play it."

"You don't play?" Vickie asked.

"Nope. My grandmother wasn't as good of a briber as you." Eva winked at her. "Logan, can you play now?" Eva begged. "Really, it would be wonderful for the piano to be used. And I have some Christmas music."

"Oh, I don't know, I'm pretty rusty," Logan said.

Vickie waved a hand in the air. "Oh, I don't believe that. You practice more than you admit. I know it. Come on, it's Christmas."

"Yes, Logan, it's Christmas." Jordan gave him a pouty look.

Logan turned and looked at Eva and she gave him the same pouty look.

"Oh, all right."

"Yay!" Eva cheered. She stood and went to the shelf and pulled out the Christmas sheet music. Her grandmother had always kept it out during the holidays. She handed it to Logan and he turned towards the piano. Vickie stood and looped her arm through Eva's as they followed him.

Eva was in awe as she watched him sit down at the instrument. He carefully set the music on the stand and opened the cover. He ran his fingers over the keys gently at first and then began to play. The notes of "Oh, Come All Ye Faithful" filled the room and Eva's heart leapt at the sound. She never considered herself a strong singer, but if Logan could be brave enough to play, she could sing along. She started the words and Vickie joined her. Soon the whole family was singing the words.

As they sang the final words to the song. Vickie gave a cheer and then squeezed Eva into a hug. "This is the most wonderful Christmas ever," she whispered in her ear.

Eva felt her heart squeeze at the words, both because her guests were happy at the inn, and because she felt like she was catching a glimpse of being part of a real family on Christmas morning. Her heart swelled as Logan began to play the next song. Without a thought, she wrapped her arms around his neck and planted a kiss on his cheek.

He had been right, this was turning out to be a wonderful Christmas.

16

*E*va bundled up in her coat, scarf and gloves. She did one last check to see if anyone needed anything before Logan tugged her out the door. "Brr," she shivered as they stepped out on the porch. But when Logan tucked her arm into his, the heat radiated through her. The crunch of their boots in the snow was the only sound as he led her down the driveway that they couldn't see and out towards the wooded area.

"Where are we going?" Eva asked.

"Just for a walk. I just thought it would be nice to take a break from everyone."

"You need that, don't you? Alone time and quiet?" Eva asked.

Logan nodded, staring off into the trees.

"Then why did you bring me along? That's not alone," she laughed. "And with me, it's definitely not quiet."

Logan wrapped his other hand over hers and held on. He seemed to think about his answer. "I think it's because I'm just comfortable with you." He grinned at her. "I'm an intro-vert, but that doesn't mean I don't like people. It just means that when I feel like I have to be "on" and act the way people think I'm supposed to, it can be tiring. But I don't feel that way with you. I feel like I don't have to try, I can just be."

"I feel that too."

"And I don't have to have it quiet, because I like listening to you talk."

Eva laughed again. "Well, I do like to talk, so that's good. But I like to hear what you think too."

He nodded. "I like to say what I'm thinking, but only if I feel like it's necessary." He cleared his throat and Eva thought he was about to say something else. But his eyes darted behind her and he froze in place. "Shh," he held up a finger to his lips. "Look," he whispered.

Eva slowly turned her head and caught a glimpse of two deer standing close to the edge of the pine tree line. She gasped and squeezed Logan's arm with her hand. They stood in silence and watched as the deer stopped and stared back at them. For several beats, no one moved and Eva held her breath. Finally the deer jumped and then ran off.

"Wow, that was amazing!" Eva didn't try to stay quiet now. "I've never seen them that close up before."

"Me either. They were beautiful."

"I wish I could have gotten a picture of that. It was a perfect Christmas scene."

"You'll just have to remember it here." Logan turned to face her and tapped her forehead with his finger. He let his finger trace down her cheek and cupped the back of her neck in his hand. Eva wrapped her arms around his waist as he leaned his head down. His lips met hers and melted away the cold of the snow. She kissed him with a passion she hadn't known before, a kiss that could only come with someone who belonged in her memories and in her heart.

When they parted, their warm breath could be seen in the cold air. And Eva smiled at him. "I won't forget the deer, even without a picture. I could never forget this moment with you."

"Me either," Logan said. He took her hand in his. "Let's keep walking."

Eva knew that she would walk with him all day if he wanted to. They made their way into the trees. Only a little way in, Logan stopped and abruptly took a turn to the right. "I think it's this way," he said.

"What is?"

"You'll see."

A short way down the path and Logan pulled them both to a stop in front of a beautiful tree. The fluffy green branches were sprinkled with snow. But what was surprising was the wheelbarrow covered in a tarp beside it. "What in the world?" Eva said. "How did that get out here?"

Logan stepped in front of her before she could pull the tarp back. He took her hands in his. "I asked Lewis if I could borrow some tools and the wheelbarrow. I wanted you to have a Christmas tree."

Eva's mouth dropped open. "What? But we have a tree at the inn, in the living room."

"I know. But that's for all your guests, and it's not just for you. I wanted you to have what your grandparents did for you. Your own private tree in your room to celebrate."

"Oh, you didn't have to do that."

"I know. But that's what makes it special."

Her heart overflowed with emotion at the thought of a tree in the room where she had celebrated Christmas with her grandparents. "Thank you," she whispered before she pressed her lips to his.

"You're welcome." He laughed. "But now you have to help me cut this tree and carry it back in the snow. So you might not want to thank me yet."

Eva laughed too. "Are you sure you don't want to pick a smaller tree? It would be easier to carry."

Logan shook his head. "Nope, this one is perfect."

She had to agree.

Logan uncovered the wheelbarrow now and pulled out a hand saw. It took him a few minutes, but he made quick work, and Eva held the top of the tree as he cut it. He covered the tools back up and promised to come for it later. Then he lifted one end while Eva grabbed onto the other. Their trip back somehow seemed much longer than their leisurely walk into the woods.

At the inn, they carried the tree straight up the stairs. Eva assumed it was Lewis who had placed the Christmas tree stand outside her door. But she pressed her back to the door and cleared her throat. "Um, maybe I should go in first. Just let me check the condition of the room."

Logan nodded and Eva barely opened the door to slip in without another word.

She was a generally neat person, but the excitement of the day had her jumping out of bed this morning. She hadn't made the bed or picked up the pajamas off the floor. She would have died if Logan had come in to see that. She was already nervous enough for him to come into her room. No one had been in there since she had moved in. It was a sacred place, off-limits to her staff and her guests. She grabbed up every stray item off the floor and put them away and then made the bed. She glanced around for anything else she might not want him to see. But other than dirty laundry, she knew she didn't care what he saw.

She swung the door wide open. "Come on in."

Logan managed to lift the tree himself, so she backed out of the way as he passed. The smell of pine needles immediately filled her room and flooded her mind with memories. She grabbed the tree stand and took it to the exact spot her grandparents had put the tree every year. Logan effortlessly placed the tree in the stand. Eva stepped back to admire it as he secured it. When he stood, he came and slipped an arm around her waist.

"What do you think?"

"It's perfect," she whispered.

He kissed her cheek. "Do you have decorations you want to put on it?"

Eva wrinkled her nose. Knowing she had used all the decorations she could find or buy on her credit card on the tree downstairs. "No. But I don't mind. I think it's beautiful the way it is." She sighed. "I didn't think of putting a tree in here this year. But thanks to you, it happened anyway. I think I'll plan to have a tree in here every Christmas from now on."

Logan stepped behind her to face the tree and wrapped both arms around her. He spoke near her ear. "I think you should."

"And what about you?" She asked. "Did you put up a Christmas tree this year?"

"Not exactly."

Eva turned in his arms and stared at him wide-eyed. "What do you mean?"

Logan scratched the back of his head. "Well, I didn't put one up at my house. It seems silly to put it up just for me. But there was one in my office."

Eva scrunched her eyebrows. "Do you spend more time in your office than your house?"

Logan looked a little guilty. "Maybe." He shrugged.

"That's not good for you either."

Logan nodded. "You're probably right." His phone dinged in his pocket before he could say anything else. He glanced at it. "It's Mom. She wants to get a family picture on Christmas day."

Eva felt disappointed and relieved at the same time. She

hated to share him, just when she was starting to learn more about him. But it also made her very aware of how close they were for him to be standing in her bedroom. "Great." She said. "Let's go. I can help with the picture. I know the perfect spot, in front of the tree."

She flung the door open and took a deep breath. One glance at Logan and she knew he was feeling the same thing as she was. She ran back to him and wrapped her arms around his neck. "Thank you for my tree," she whispered in his ear. She pressed a kiss to his cheek before taking his hand and pulling him out the door.

17

*L*ogan's heart felt like it was floating through the air as he followed Eva down the steps. His mom had been right about this being the best Christmas ever. But he had never felt this way about anyone before. He kept waiting for a warning signal to go off in his brain, telling him to slow down and back away. It always did when he started to open up to someone. But with Eva, he didn't feel that at all. He only felt comfort and peace.

"Come on Logan, we're waiting for you," his mom called out.

Vickie, Robert, and Jordan all stood in the living room.

"Let's take it in front of the tree. Here Logan, let me have your phone." Eva held out her hand as she directed them.

The family moved in front of the tree. "Come on now, move closer," Eva said. "Vickie and Robert, scoot together, and Jordan, you go on one side and Logan on the other." They did as they were told and they smiled as Eva said, "Say 'cheese.' " She snapped a few frames, then swiped through them. "These look nice. It will be a great family memory."

Vickie stepped close to look over her shoulder. "Oh yes,

those are perfect." She reached for the phone. "Now, Eva, let me take one of you and Logan in front of the tree." Eva held up her hand as if she might protest. Logan knew that was pointless.

His smile was even bigger than before and Eva stepped close and he tucked her under his arm.

"Say 'Merry Christmas,'" Vickie called out.

"Merry Christmas!" Eva and Logan said.

"Perfect!" Vickie said, smiling at the photo on the screen. "You should put this one in your office, Logan."

"I just might do that."

"And the one of the family is perfect for a Christmas card. Or maybe you could use it in next year's Christmas issues with a note saying Merry Christmas from the Bradford Family. It's always nice for readers to know we're still a family-owned company."

Logan flinched. He couldn't see Eva's face. But he heard her say, "Family owned company?"

"Yes, that's right. But let me see the other pictures." He hoped that would distract her enough until he could talk to her alone.

When he saw the look Eva gave him, he knew that wasn't going to work. "I thought Logan worked for a magazine."

Jordan let out a laugh. "That's kind of true. Except it's not one magazine, it's hundreds."

"Jordan," Logan said through clenched teeth.

"Oh, sorry, he doesn't work for them either. He runs the whole publishing company."

Eva didn't hide her emotions. Her eyes flashed with anger. "And who owns the company?" She looked straight into Logan's eyes.

He blinked several times, trying to think of a way to soften this, but nothing came to mind, except the truth. "Our family."

Eva nodded slowly and then turned away from him. He could practically hear that she forced a smile as she said. "Excuse me, I need to check on a few things. Enjoy your afternoon Bradford Family."

Logan winced as she punctuated the last words.

Vickie gave him a sympathetic look. "I guess you hadn't told her that piece of information."

"No, I hadn't. Thanks, Jordan."

Jordan held his hands up in the air. "Hey, it's not my fault you didn't tell her. How was I supposed to know it was a secret?"

"We discussed this before we came on this trip. I didn't want anyone to know who our family was on this vacation."

Jordan shrugged. "Yeah, I remember. I just figured if you actually liked this girl, you would have told her the truth."

Logan wanted to punch him. But he knew his brother was right. He should have told her before now.

Vickie patted his arm. "I'm sure it will be alright. Just go talk to her."

Logan took a deep breath. He wasn't as sure as his mom, but he knew he needed to go find Eva. He walked with purpose out of the living room and into the kitchen. Eva was there, filling the coffee machine, even though there was a full pot of coffee already. "Eva, can we talk, please?"

She didn't turn around, but he saw her shrug her shoulders. "Why? You didn't want to tell me who you really are, so what is there to say now?" She slammed the lid to the coffee maker down and turned to face him. "What happened to being yourself and being comfortable with me?"

"I wanted to tell you. I started to, more than once, but something always interrupted and I just wanted to find the right way and the right words."

"I think the right words would have just been the truth.

So what was this anyway?" She pointed back and forth between them. "Just a vacation fling with a secret identity?"

"No, no, not at all. I just didn't want to tell anyone who our family was on this trip. It just complicates things, and people just…" he paused, trying to word it delicately. "People just treat us differently when they know."

"Why? Because you own a bunch of magazines?"

Logan cleared his throat. He knew that now was his only chance for complete honesty. "Because of our money."

Eva's mouth fell open and she backed up into the corner. She crossed her arms. "I assumed that anyone who could afford four rooms at the inn for two weeks at Christmas had a little bit of money. But I didn't think much of it. What do you mean? How do people treat you differently? And how much money do you have, anyway?"

Logan watched her reaction and saw how her eyes grew wide when he said, "Billions."

"You're joking."

"I'm not." He shook his head. "My great grandfather started the company as a small-town newspaper, but as it has grown, the family acquired more and more publications." He shrugged. "It adds up."

"And you couldn't tell me that? How did you think I would act?"

"It's not how you would act. It's how others have acted in the past. I've had many women want to date me. And it's taken me too long to learn they weren't interested in Logan. Only in the Bradford part of my name and the money that goes with it."

Eva's cheeks turned red and her eyes flashed with anger. "And you thought I would be the same way? Do you think I can't take care of myself? I don't need your money."

"No, no, I didn't think that. We decided not to tell anyone before I met you. I didn't mean to keep it from you this long."

Eva held up a hand. "Don't. Don't make excuses now. I don't know what I thought was going to happen. But if you can't trust me enough to tell me who you are and the truth about your family, you must not think very much of me. I'll tell you this, my grandparents kept this inn going by their own two hands. And I have done the same since the day I took over. And I'll keep doing it. I don't need your billions of dollars. And I definitely don't need you to pretend you care and then go back to your life and forget about me after Christmas."

"Eva, I..."

"No. Let's just not. What did you think would happen? You're leaving tomorrow, aren't you?"

Logan nodded.

Eva sighed. "I'm not sure what I was hoping for. But I know you have to go back to your job and your responsibilities. So let's not pretend we were more than we were. You go on back to your family. They might be the only people who really know you." She turned and walked towards the doorway. She just turned her chin over her shoulder as she said, "I have an inn to run."

Logan collapsed onto the stool and let his head fall into his hands. This was the exact opposite of what he wanted. He had been so afraid of opening up and telling her the truth because she might take advantage and hurt him. Instead he had hurt her by keeping a secret.

Now what? Eva was right, of course. He was leaving tomorrow. And he had a job and responsibilities. He wasn't planning to walk away from them. And he lived more than two hours away from here. Was he going to quit and move so they could pursue a relationship? Certainly he had made it clear how important his family and his job were. So that wasn't something he could consider.

Logan sighed. Maybe she was right. Maybe this was the

best Christmas ever. But maybe that's all it could ever be. He stood and walked from the kitchen. The sun was setting outside the window, and Christmas was drawing to a close. This trip was about to be over. And his relationship with Eva was over with it.

18

*E*va tapped her finger on the keyboard of her computer without typing anything. She had been staring at the reservation list for January for several minutes, but she still wasn't sure what it said. She had an email asking about dates in January and another requesting a booking in March. But all Eva could do was stare at the screen. She had changed the names back from the Christmas themed rooms to the authors' names, and the Charles Dickens room was taunting her. It had been hard enough to be in the room clearing out all the Christmas decorations. It was as if she could smell Logan, even imagine him in the room. But now every time she looked for an available room, it was as if the words "Charles Dickens" glowed from her screen and she could hear Logan saying, "My favorite author."

She shook her head to rid herself of the memory. Maybe he had told her his favorite author and favorite dessert, but he had left out enough important details to know that he wasn't being honest with her. He had been gone for two weeks now, and she hadn't heard a word from him. Not that she expected to after she told him to go back to his real life.

She had only wondered every day if she had done the right thing. But she wasn't willing to risk starting something with someone who hadn't told her the truth. Someone who could walk out of her life as easily as he had walked in. Besides, it could never work. He had a company to run, and she had to stay here and keep her grandparents' inn alive.

It hurt now, but she felt certain it would hurt more if she let herself get even more attached. Just the memory of sitting around the Christmas tree with Logan and his family caused her to ache. For a brief moment she had let herself believe she might be part of a real family. But it slipped away, and she was going to have to live with that.

She blew out a big breath and told herself to focus on the inn. It only took a few minutes once she gave it her full attention to check the reservations and respond to the emails. Her inn would be full for the next three months. The reviews from the Christmas guests were coming in, and their social media was getting a lot of attention. Eva sighed. She knew she should be happy, thrilled even. Her dream of reviving her grandparents' inn was coming true. At this rate she would be able to pay off the repairs and her credit card and really get the business going. She was happy. But there was a shadow over it.

A shadow named Logan Bradford. He had made this her best, and worst, Christmas all at the same time.

She didn't know if she would ever get over that.

LOGAN LEFT THE MEETING WITH SEVERAL OF HIS EDITORS. HE rubbed his forehead where a dull ache had started about an hour ago. He wanted to say it was because he hadn't had any coffee that morning. But he knew the real reason. It was the same reason as every day.

Regret.

He had spent weeks thinking about his time at the inn and playing it in his head over and over again. How could he have done things differently? He played it out, telling her the truth, with her accepting him and treating him the same as always. But it was too late for that now.

He walked into his office and shut the door behind him. He had smiled and nodded and agreed to ideas for the entire meeting. Now he was exhausted and wanted peace and quiet. He could process better that way.

Logan knew he should be thinking about the decisions they had discussed in the meeting. But his mind was elsewhere.

How could he ever apologize to Eva in a way that she would understand? There had to be a way to get back to her. Logan sighed. Even if she could forgive him, there was still the issue of distance. He was here in Charlotte, where he planned to stay for the rest of his life. And Eva was over two hours away in Asheville, where she wanted to keep running her grandparents' inn. Both of them had a family legacy to uphold. He couldn't ask her to leave that any more than he could leave his own.

There was a knock on his door and he looked up. There wasn't an appointment on his calendar. "Come in," he called out.

The door opened and his mom and dad walked in. "Hey," Logan stood, concern flooding him. He watched as his brother followed his parents in. Logan walked around his desk and kissed his mom on the cheek, and shook hands with his dad. "Jordan," he said, giving a curt nod to him. "Is something wrong?"

Vickie patted him on the arm. "Let's all sit down and talk."

A knot formed in his stomach as he led them to the couch

in his office. His parents took a seat, but Jordan remained standing. Logan sat in the armchair adjacent to the couch.

"Son," Robert began. "We know you're disappointed over the way Christmas ended."

Logan held up a hand. "Dad, please. I don't really want to talk about it."

"That's what we're here for. That and a few other things."

Logan sighed and settled into the chair.

Vickie picked up the conversation. "We had a wonderful time, and I'm sorry it ended badly for you." She waved a hand in the air. "But first we need to talk about Jordan."

"What about Jordan?" Logan scoffed.

"I talked with Mom and Dad about my plans."

"Your plans to quit the family business?"

"Logan," Robert's voice was stern. "You need to listen."

"You didn't let me explain anything. I know you think I'm lazy and a terrible employee. But the truth is, I have no desire to work for a publishing company."

Logan forced his hand through his hair. "That's ridiculous. We own the company, it's who our family is and what we do. And you can have any job you want. You can work in marketing, or photography, or writing. You can take out the garbage if you want."

"I don't want to work for the publishing company."

Logan felt his anger rising. "And why not?"

"Because I don't want to just be a Bradford and follow what everyone in our family has always done." Jordan paused and took a deep breath. "I want to start my own company."

"What?" Logan would have been less shocked if Jordan said he wanted to be a circus clown. "What kind of company? You don't even like coming to work."

Jordan grinned. "I don't like coming to work at a magazine publisher. I know, I've been a bad employee, and I really am sorry for that. But it's because I have ideas and plans for what I really want to do. I want to start a non-profit."

Logan squinted, not sure he was hearing this right. "What kind of non-profit?"

"I'd like to work with international healthcare."

Logan was speechless. He certainly hadn't expected that. "But you're not a doctor."

"I don't have to be to run an organization. Remember when I went to Africa?"

"Sure."

"I met a team of doctors there. They were only there short term, but I learned a lot about what they do and how badly they need healthcare workers. I didn't go to medical school, but I can raise money and send supplies and organize people to go and help."

Logan rubbed his chin. That was the most mature thing he'd ever heard from Jordan. He thought he'd spent his time abroad in tourist destinations. Not learning about worldwide health needs. "I'm guessing you're going to need money to get started."

Jordan grinned. "I've already spoken with several of your business connections about supporting our efforts."

"And you'll be asking us for the same?"

Jordan's gaze turned serious. "I'm not asking for a hand-out. I have an inheritance and if that's what I use to get this started, so be it. I can move into a one-bedroom apartment and eat peanut butter sandwiches if that's what it takes."

Logan had never seen this side of his brother. "You're determined then?"

Jordan nodded firmly.

"And you approve of this?" Logan looked from one parent to the other.

Vickie smiled and Robert spoke for both of them. "I've had my reservations, and I think he'll need guidance. But I'm pleased with his idea, and I think he's thought it through long enough to make a decision for himself."

Logan nodded. "All right then. I'm happy for you, Jordan." He stood and reached out to shake hands with his brother.

"Thanks," Jordan said. He dropped his gaze. "I know we haven't always seen eye-to-eye. You were right when you said I've been irresponsible. But seeing these people in need really changed me. I want to do better."

Logan reached out and ruffled Jordan's hair. "I think you're going to turn out alright."

Jordan pushed his hand away, but smiled good-naturedly.

Vickie stood to join them and looped her hands through each of their arms. "I'm proud of you both, and happy to see you agreeing on something." She turned to her oldest son. "Now Logan, we need to fix this problem with you and Eva."

Logan whipped his head around to look at her. "What? No, Mom, we're not talking about this."

"Yes, we are," Vickie said.

Jordan jumped in, "Yeah, I hear you've been moping around ever since Christmas."

Logan wanted to argue, but he knew it was true. He shrugged his shoulders. "There's nothing to be done."

Vickie let go of them and waved a hand in the air. "Sure there is. There's always something to be done. Have you talked to her?"

Logan shook his head. "She doesn't want to hear from me."

"You just have to find the right thing to say. You hurt her feelings by keeping something from her. So now you need to show her you really care. What's the most important thing to her?"

Logan didn't miss a beat. "Her grandparents' inn."

"There you go. Do something to show you care about that too."

Logan stared at his mom as if she had lost her mind. But slowly an idea began to form. He nodded at her as he thought of a plan. "Maybe you're right."

Vickie laughed. "Of course I'm right. Now go after her."

"I'll see you all later. I've got some calls to make."

19

*E*va had been straightening up in the living room. There was a never ending list of things to be done at the Inn. But she stopped to watch slow flakes falling outside the window. She smiled, but the snow only reminded her of Logan.

What was he doing now? Had he thought of her at all since he left? For the millionth time, she wondered if she could have done things differently. She pressed her palm to the cold glass and whispered a prayer for help and wisdom. She moved from the window and her eyes landed on the portrait of her grandparents. She sighed as she thought of their love and their happiness here in the inn, the dream they built together.

"Together," Eva whispered. Her eyes flooded with tears as a realization washed over her.

It wasn't about the inn. It never had been. The inn was their dream, not because of the inn, but because they worked at it together. Grandpa had worked hard for years, leaving his wife every morning, but his wish was to be with her all day. They sacrificed a lot to get the inn going, but they did it because they worked together.

Eva traced the photograph with her finger. "Your legacy isn't the inn. It's the love you had for each other. And for me. She kissed the tips of her fingers and then pressed it to the picture. She knew in that moment that what they would want for her was to live a life she loved, with someone she loved.

That was worth the sacrifice.

Now she could only pray that one day she could have the kind of love they had.

EVA HADN'T MOVED ALL MORNING. THE PHONE HAD BEEN ringing off the hook, and her online reservation requests were through the roof. "Sharon," she called out, with the phone on her shoulder and her hands poised over the keyboard. "Do you think you could bring me a cup of coffee when you get a second?"

Sharon smiled and nodded. "Busy day, huh?"

"It's unbelievable! I guess the reviews are coming in. But I didn't expect it to explode quite like this."

Lewis came around the corner. "Wonder why there was such a boom today, though."

"I don't know, but we're booked for eight months out. This keeps up and we'll be booked for the rest of the year!"

The bell over the front door rang and Eva looked up expecting a guest. She pasted on a smile and tried not to look frazzled. She was relieved to see her friend. "Katie, hey. What are you doing here?"

Katie's eyes were wide, and she shut the door behind her and leaned back against it. "Have you seen it yet?"

"What?" Eva leaned sideways trying to peer out the window. "Is something out there?"

"No, the magazine, have you seen it?"

"Magazine?" Eva's mind went blank except for the only thing that came to mind with that word. The Bradford Family. "What are you talking about?"

Katie quickly moved to the desk and plopped a magazine on the desk. Eva looked down and saw the cover of *Country Travel Magazine*. The words "Five Inns For a Perfect, Relaxing Vacation" graced the front in bold letters. Eva scrunched her eyebrows. "And?" she said.

"Open it," Katie said, but didn't wait for Eva, and turned the pages at lightning speed. When she reached the spot she was looking for, she stopped and pointed.

Eva gasped. Her hands went to her chest and she could barely catch her breath. There on the pages of the magazine, in beautiful, full color was her inn. She couldn't make out all the words in her shock, but she caught "Wonderful," "Relaxing," "Cozy," and "Charming."

"How? Why? Who?" Eva managed to squeak out. She felt frozen in place.

"You didn't know? I thought maybe you just didn't tell me as a surprise." Katie said. "But Eva, this is amazing! Look at these pictures!" Katie pointed again to the pages, then a confused look came over her face. "Wait, if you didn't know, how did they get these images? Are they from the website?"

Eva leaned over and scrutinized them. "I don't think so."

"I might have an idea about that," a voice said.

Eva squeezed her eyes shut and stood perfectly still. It couldn't be. And yet, it had to be. Who else could have done this? And she knew that voice beyond a shadow of a doubt. She opened her eyes and slowly turned towards the living room. He stood in the doorway. "Logan," she whispered.

He stepped in the room and Eva's breath caught in her

throat. She was vaguely aware that everyone else made their way out of the room. "You?" She pointed at the magazine still laying on the desk. "You did this?"

He nodded. "I did."

"But how did you get the photos?"

"Lewis. He let the photographer in when you were gone to town."

"Oh," Eva nodded.

"I know you don't need my money or my help. But I also knew that I could help you reach your dream. This place is important to you, and that makes it important to me."

"But I don't understand. I thought your magazines were put together months in advance."

"They are," he said, still slowly moving towards her. "But when you're in charge, there are strings to pull."

Eva bit her lip. He had done this for her. He had stopped production, and made changes, probably expensive ones, for her. "The phone hasn't stopped ringing all day. We're going to start booking for next year."

Logan smiled. "That's great."

"Great? It's incredible! I hoped I could get the inn off the ground, but we're up in the sky. I've got a waiting list and deposits coming in. I'll be able to fully staff the inn."

Logan stood right in front of her now, he looked like he wanted to reach out for her, but he restrained himself. "Does that mean you might be able to take some time off?"

Her eyes met his and she couldn't look away. Didn't want to look away. "Depends on what for."

Logan took her hand in his now. "Eva, I handled everything wrong. I have played it over and over in my mind, and I wish I could go back and just tell you everything from the beginning. I was afraid and I thought the only way to stay safe was to keep my life private." He stopped and let out a big breath. "But I learned that sometimes you need to take a risk, and you need to put it all out there and see what happens."

Eva's heart threatened to pound out of her chest. She pressed her lips together as he laced his fingers through hers.

"So that's what I'm here for now. I wanted your inn in the magazine, because it's perfect. Every word in there is true. It's relaxing and cozy, and I've never been happier anywhere in my life. Other people need to see that. And I want you to have all the success you can imagine here. But I also want you to know me. Yes, my family owns a large magazine publishing company. My great-grandfather started it, and it's been passed down through the generations to me. My family has money, a lot of money. But I prefer to not think about that too much or talk about it a lot. I like my job and I like working hard at it." He stopped and gazed into her eyes for several moments. "But I also really like you. Eva, you are kind and caring, you're fun, and I like to listen to you talk and ask questions, and I admire how hard you've worked for this inn. I don't want to keep secrets from you. I want you to know everything about me. And I'd like to know about you too. I want to put myself out there and give this a chance."

Eva sucked in a breath. "I think that's the most I've ever heard you say at once." She laughed.

Logan laughed too. "It may be the most I've ever said at once, other than meetings. But I mean every word."

"I like you too, Logan. I like that you're a little quiet, it means I know you really thought about what you said before you said it. And I believe you."

"I never meant to hurt you."

"I believe you."

"I'm still sorry I kept anything from you."

"Me too. But thank you for saying it."

"Do you think we can give this a chance?"

Eva sighed then. "Logan, I want to. Oh, so badly. I've

missed you and wished I could talk to you every day since Christmas. But you have your life and I have mine, and they're not remotely close. How can we make it work?"

Logan cleared his throat and squared his shoulders. "I've thought about that. A lot. I would never ask you to leave the inn. It's your family history and I know that's important."

"I've thought about the inn a lot too. You know I thought that the inn was what was important to my grandparents, but the more I'm here, the more I realize that it's not really about the inn. I loved being here with them, and they loved being here. But they would have been happy anywhere as long as they were together."

"Maybe there's a compromise for us. Maybe we do long distance for a while and see how it goes." A grin spread across his face. "But I have a feeling I won't like that very much for very long."

Eva blushed.

"But I can work remotely some of the time, and if you're able to hire help at the inn, maybe we can find a schedule that works for us."

Eva nodded slowly. "Okay."

"Okay, you think that can work? Or okay, you want to give this a chance?"

Eva smiled. "Okay. To all of it."

Logan reached for her and picked her up in his arms, he spun her in a circle before he set her down. He cupped her face in his hands and kissed her.

Eva smiled as she leaned back to look at him. Just a month ago, she had stood in front of her inn, expecting a great holiday. But she couldn't have known then the gift that Christmas would be. Now she knew she could look forward to the future, counting the man in front of her as one of her many blessings.

EPILOGUE

*E*va smoothed her hands over her dress as she looked at herself in the mirror. Giggles bubbled out along with the excitement flowing through her. She glanced at the clock and wondered if he was here yet.

Dating Logan long distance had been even better than she could have imagined. They talked on the phone constantly and saw each other most weekends. Sometimes Logan came to visit, but with the inn so full most of the time, he had to find a nearby hotel. So more often than not, Eva drove to Charlotte and stayed at his parents' house. The weeks flew by as they spent every available moment together.

Now the summer was drawing to an end, Eva couldn't believe before long she would be pulling out the Christmas decorations again. But she wouldn't think about that tonight. Tonight Logan would be here to take her to dinner, and she wouldn't think of anything else.

Her black dress showed off her figure and her heels clicked across the hardwood as she made her way down the stairs. She gasped when she saw the man who held her heart waiting at the bottom.

She picked up her pace and when she reached him, she wrapped her arms around his waist. He tipped her chin up and kissed her. It was everything a kiss should be when you hadn't seen someone in a week.

"Hi," Eva said.

"Hi," Logan kissed her again.

When he released her, Eva said, "Are you ready to go?"

"In a minute. I have something for you first. Come on." He tucked her hand in his and pulled her towards the kitchen.

She looked up and saw a large, wrapped box with a giant bow sitting on the counter. "What's this?"

"Open it," Logan grinned.

"It's not my birthday."

"I know. Just open it."

Eva stepped to the counter and gripped the wrapping paper. She didn't waste any time and pulled it off with a flourish. She started laughing when she saw the picture of a large, commercial sized coffee maker on the box. "I can't believe you got this! The other one still works."

Logan smiled. "I've replaced the fuse twice since Christmas. It was time."

Eva turned and raised her eyebrows at him. "But now I won't be able to call you and ask you to drive all the way here to fix the coffee maker."

"Is that what you keep me around for?"

Eva lifted one shoulder. "I'll never tell."

Logan stepped close and pulled her into his arms. "I think it's best that we replace the coffee maker. I can't always be available for coffee maker repair, and you need a reliable machine here."

Eva poked her lip out in a pout. "It's not important enough for you to come all the way here?"

Logan took a deep breath. "Actually, I had a different idea."

"Let's hear it."

"I think that your inn manager should handle the coffee maker. But if you want, we can take the old one back to Charlotte and I'll be around to fix it anytime."

Eva tilted her head and drew her eyebrows down.

"Eva, these past few months have been wonderful. I wanted us to get to know each other with no secrets, and the only thing I've learned is that I love you more and more every day. I love the way you get that look on your face when you're really thinking about something, and I love the sound of your laugh. Mostly I love how you care about people, and how you're passionate about whatever you do." He cleared his throat. "But I don't want to keep going like we're going."

"You don't?" Eva's voice was breathless.

"No, it's time for something new. I never knew that I could be so sure that I wanted to spend the rest of my life with someone. Someone that I know, that I trust, and that I love with all my heart. But I know that now. I love you, Eva, and I want nothing more than to spend the rest of my life with you. Eva Parks, will you marry me?"

Eva blinked away the tears that had pooled in her eyes. "I love you, Logan. I was scared too, for a long time, to let anyone in. The only people that had been steady in my life were my grandparents. I knew I could never commit to someone unless I felt like it would be a love like theirs. I hate that they never met you, because I know they would approve. And I know that I can spend the rest of my life loving you. Yes, I'll marry you!"

Logan pressed his lips to hers. She held his face in her hands and giggled as she kissed him back. When they parted, he reached into his pocket and pulled out a small black box.

Eva gasped when he opened it to reveal the diamond ring

inside. It was a perfect solitaire. Not too flashy or screaming that he had money, but a ring that he must have picked out just for her. He slipped it on her finger before he kissed her once more.

"Now," he said. "I think we can go to dinner."

"Oh, I practically forgot about dinner."

"Well, I would say we could skip it, but I think my parents would be disappointed."

"They're here?"

He nodded. "Mom, Dad, and Jordan are meeting us at the restaurant."

Eva lit up like a Christmas tree. She grabbed his hand and pulled him towards the door. "Let's get going then. I can't wait to share our news with the whole family."

"Our family," Logan said.

"Yes, our family. Forever, right?"

"Forever."

ABOUT THE AUTHOR

Hannah Jo Abbott is not just a writer, but a wife, a mom of four, a homeschool teacher, a daughter, a sister, and a friend. She loves writing stories about life, love, and the grace of God. And she finds inspiration and encouragement from reading the stories others share. Hannah lives with her husband and children in Sweet Home Alabama.

For updates on her writing and to receive a FREE novella, sign up for Hannah Jo's newsletters at hannahjoabbott.com/mailinglist.html

Made in the USA
Columbia, SC
01 November 2024

45475548R00071